CW00841070

The Dance Macabre

Short Stories & Flash Fiction

by

Claire Casey

COPYRIGHT

OTHER WORKS

Goddess of the Night

Northlore Series: Volume 1 (Folklore)

King and the Spider

The Winter Queen

Northlore Series: Volume 2 (Mythos)

EDITED & INTRODUCED

The Weaver Poet: Songs and Poems by Robert Tannahill

Lines Written on a Summer Evening: Poems by Alexander Wilson

ACKNOWLEDGEMENTS

As always, a big thank you goes to the Nordland Crew. I love having a group of fellow writers that supports each other. May that long continue.

To Michelle Lowe, for helping with the re-editing of The Dance Macabre, and for helping to kick it into shape.

To the writers group at Braehead. Thank you for letting me join, and for allowing me to throw some story ideas at you, without thinking that I was a complete weirdo.

The painting used on the cover of this collection was painted by Phillippe de Champaigne.

The title "Is This the Real Life?" is taken from Bohemian Rhapsody, written by Freddie Mercury.

Dedication

As always, this is dedicated to my mum and dad. You have had to face so much, but that never stopped you from wanting to see me do well. I can't repay that.

To Ann and Donna, Anne from Kilwinning, Uncle Jelly and Michelle L. Thank you for the support. It will always be appreciated.

Journey

Someone once told me a journey of a thousand miles begins with a single step.

It is that first, tiny step that is the most terrifying. What will happen? What will others think? What if you fail? There will always be that tiny voice - in the back of your mind - filled with doubt. It whispers to you, telling you to remain where you are safe. Where you will never get hurt.

Playing safe will be of no consolation, when you are lying on your death bed, with nothing more to show for your life, than fears and regrets. There is a whole world out there. It is waiting for you. Get outside your comfort zone and push those boundaries. Question everything you have been so certain of. Never accept what others tell you, without putting it to the test.

People have the nasty habit of lying.

Why not take the road less travelled and prove your doubters wrong? Leave them behind and allow them to rock in your wake. Begin the journey of a lifetime and quit the job you hate. Never look back. No regrets. No fears.

Never wonder what could have been. Keep your gaze set on the next adventure and continue to wonder about what lies over the furthest horizon.

Life is not about going to the grave in a pristine and perfect body, no matter what others may try to tell you. Life is about sliding in sideways, screaming

—

"Fuck, that was fun!"

Doopler-ganger

"Gunn, can you check the tracking system?" Commander Ashley Boyle asked. "It was playing up while you were doing your spacewalk. I stopped it from playing silly buggers, but it doesn't hurt to have someone else look at it."

The *Mars Orbiter*, the space station that had been their home for the past six months, was spartan. It was too cramped for any form of luxury to be on board. The basics were all they had been given. They were there to work, not to enjoy themselves. Scientific equipment filled every available space, with a variety of machines beeping as they recorded the planet below them.

"Give me a few minutes. I'm just finishing this experiment," Sub-Commander Morag Gunn replied, as she glanced up from her scribbled notes.

With a nod and a smile, Boyle walked past her, grateful to whoever had invented artificial gravity. She could remember the footage she had watched in astronaut training and it was enough to make her shudder. Every video she had seen was filled with images of her predecessors floating through their shuttles. Everything else had to be strapped down before they drifted off through the orbiter.

It looked ridiculous and impractical. Boyle could not understand how those old astronauts continued to smile through it all.

Coming to a porthole, she paused for a moment. Mars hung in the darkness of space, filling the view from the orbiter. It was not as red as people thought it would be. As close as they were, it looked more of a dirty reddish-brown. The environment on the planet surface was still too harsh for human life, but that would not stop the attempts to colonise the planet.

It was being billed as the next great step for humanity. Boyle was certain that there were those working on the problem of the surface, to turn it all into a paradise. There would be a series of politicians, private individuals, and business people who would make a fortune from the colonisation process.

Boyle walked through the rest of the space station. The gravity situation had improved, but the lack of space remained the same. Everything was crammed in and every nook and cranny had been put to some use. The doors to each sleeping compartment had its own, separate locking mechanism that would kick in with the entering of the right code. She was the only one who knew the codes.

There was always something going on. Things weren't always going wrong, but that did not mean that there wasn't something demanding her attention. Right at that moment, the daily update with mission control was the next task on her list.

Sitting down at the cramped desk in the corner that was the communication area, Boyle watched as the computer screen in front of her flickered into life. The familiar face of Joe Turner, the head of mission control, appeared on the screen. He sat in his office, which was just off the main floor of mission control. Joe looked frazzled as always, surrounded by piles of paperwork. He had never as not the boss who made running mission control easy. Somehow, he always got the job done.

Looking up from the file he was reading, Joe cleared his throat and he turned up the volume on his computer, allowing Boyle to hear him. Joe continued, with a voice that had been strained by too many cigarettes. "Good evening *Mars Orbiter*."

"Good evening Joe. How are things back home?" Boyle asked.

"Same shit, different day. What about yourselves? How are things on the orbiter?"

"Gunn will send her test results to you, ASAP. Don't ask me what she may have discovered, as I can never read her handwriting and she is vague when I ask her," Boyle laughed. "I'm guessing you have been picking up on the increase in solar flares."

The connection cracked and the screen froze. Hissing in frustration, Boyle had times when she hated technology. It was meant to make their lives easier, but she suspected that it was developing a mind of its own. She was certain that it only wanted to do its own thing. The connection righted itself and she could hear Joe again, with no interference.

"Sorry Joe, I didn't catch what you said there. The connection went haywire."

"That's all right. I said we have been picking up on the increase in solar activity. We're keeping an eye on it. I also wanted to remind you and Gunn that it will only be three more days until you will be heading back to Earth," Joe added.

Boyle smiled at the idea. "Oh, to have a proper bath. Hot water, bubbles and a glass of wine. That's enough to make my day. A good meal also wouldn't go amiss either."

"Right, if there isn't anything else, I will speak to you again tomorrow," Joe told her. "Same bat time, same bat channel."

As Boyle gave a joking salute, they both signed off. Heading back to where she had left Gunn, Boyle found her sitting back down at the controls of the shuttle.

"The tracking system's working fine. There's no problems there. There must have just been a glitch," Gunn stated.

Something banged on the side of the orbiter. Jumping at the sound, Boyle was certain that it sounded like someone was hitting on the side of the shuttle. Looking at each other, neither of them had to say a word for them to understand the others fear and confusion.

"What the fuck was that?" Gunn questioned. "We're the only ones up here."

Walking over to the porthole next to the airlock, they both looked out.

There was someone outside. Whoever it was, they were wearing one of their spacesuits. The figure outside of the orbiter lifted their first and banged on the outside of the airlock.

14

Turning on the intercom, Boyle spoke to the astronaut, her voice shaking, despite her best efforts. "Who are you? How did you get here?"

"Stop taking the piss, Boyle. It's Gunn. I've just finished my space-walk, so hurry up and let me in. The oxygen in this suit is running low."

Looking at the woman next to her, Boyle struggled to speak. Gunn couldn't drag her gaze away from the porthole. Neither of them could register what was taking place. Pressing the button that worked the airlock, it hissed and clunked, allowing the other into float into the antechamber. It would take a few moments before the other astronaut would be able to get inside the orbiter.

Pressing the lock for the airlock, Boyle looked at Gunn. They needed to buy themselves time.

"If only they allowed us to have guns up here," Gunn stated, in a hoarse whisper.

Keeping her eyes focused on the airlock, Boyle answered. "Guns would be the last thing that we would need up here. What do you think would happen if people started losing their minds up on a mission like this and there were weapons lying about the place? We're in a frigging metal canister that's floating through space."

Taking the initiative, Boyle unlocked the airlock. The inner door of the airlock hissed open, allowing who was inside it to stride into the orbiter.

"Boyle, I still have my results and notes to write up for mission control. I'll get onto it as soon as I can," a familiar voice stated as the figure strode into the *Mars Orbiter*. "I'm sure that they will be chomping at the bit."

"Stop right there," Boyle barked at the woman.

The other woman slowly turned around. Boyle struggled to hide her shock as the woman removed the helmet of her spacesuit. If she hadn't already known that Gunn was standing right beside her, Boyle would have sworn that the woman she was now looking at, was her friend and colleague.

"What the fuck is going on?" the other woman whispered.

Gunn and her doppelgänger stared at each other, neither of them moving, or able to speak. Neither of them was able, or willing to accept what they were seeing with their own eyes.

"You will be coming with me. You will be secured in one of the sleeping cabins until we figure out what the fuck is going on," Boyle told her, taking the doppelgänger by her upper arm.

"I'm the real Gunn. You have to believe me," the second woman pleaded.

"I don't know who the hell you are, or how the fuck you got here, but I am not willing to take any risks. Gunn has been with me for hours," Boyle hissed.

Marching the doppelgänger through the space station, Boyle forcing her into the sleeping chamber. There was no struggle - just a cold acceptance. If she had been Gunn, she would have fought, to prove who she really was. Boyle knew that Gunn was not the sort to allow herself to be forced into a makeshift prison cell, no questions asked.

Pushing the doppelgänger into the cabin, Boyle growled at her. "You will stay in here, until I say otherwise."

"You have to believe me. I have no idea who, or what that woman is, but I am Gunn," the other woman continued. "We've been working together for years, on different projects. We've been up her for nearly six months and we're going home soon."

"I have two women who appear to be the same person, in a metal tube floating in space. What kind of position do you think that puts me in? I'm not taking any chances," Boyle asked.

Closing the door, Boyle punched the code into the locking mechanism. She had no idea what she was to do next. There certainly wasn't anything in the rulebook to cover this sort of thing. Walking back to where she had left Gunn, her thoughts racing. Seeing the sombre look on her friend's face, Boyle didn't have to hear what she had to say to know what she was thinking. Boyle knew what they had to do. It was their only option.

"We will keep her locked up until we are heading back to Earth," Boyle told her.

"We will be bringing her back with us?"

"We can't just leave her here. We need to figure out who she is and what she's up to. We will just need to hold tight, until it is time for us to head home."

"I hope that you are doing the right thing," Gunn answered.

Walking over to one of the portholes, Gunn looked outside. When she pulled back, Boyle felt her heart sink even further.

"What is it?" Boyle questioned.

"This can't be happening."

"What? What's happening?" Boyle demanded. Shaking her head, Gunn looked at her friend. Her eyes were filled with fear and confusion, as she stepped back from the porthole.

"The stars are disappearing," Gunn whispered.

Going to the porthole, Boyle stared out into the darkness. At first, she could not see it. The stars still filled the darkness. Frowning, she realised that something wasn't right. One by one, the stars were disappearing, leaving nothing in their place, but black space.

Looking back at Gunn, Boyle stammered. "How can that be happening?"

"I have no idea, but it has to have something to do with that doppelgänger."

"Come in Mission Control," Boyle said, sitting in the communication area. She felt uncomfortable, knowing that the doppelgänger was in the cabin directly behind. With a shiver running down her spine, Boyle put that thought to the back of her mind. "This is *Mars Orbiter*."

"Yes, *Mars Orbiter*. We weren't expecting you to contact us again until tomorrow. How can we help you?"

The face that greeted Boyle was new. Who-ever he was, he was young. Almost too young. Boyle was certain that he didn't look old enough to have left university.

"I need to report that we have had something of an incident up here."

"What kind of incident?"

"Someone has appeared outside the orbiter. We have no idea who she is, or how she got her, but she is claiming to be Gunn," Boyle told her. "She is Gunn's double."

Making some noises of agreement, the young man scribbled away. Looking up from his notes, he smiled at Boyle, as if waiting for Boyle to continue.

"I'm curious. Where's Joe Turner? Has he gone home already?" Boyle asked.

"Joe Turner?" the man frowned. "I don't know of anyone by that name in mission control."

"I spoke to him today."

Holding an index finger up, asking for a moment, the man disappeared. After a few moments, he appeared once again, looking very uncertain.

"I've spoken with some of the others on duty. There has never been someone working in mission control called Joe Turner," he told Boyle. "Maybe you should see one of the organisations psychiatrists when you get back. The stresses of being in space so long must be getting to you."

"I will not be seeing a psychiatrist. I can assure you that there is a Joe Turner. I have been working with him for years. He manages mission control."

In frustration, Boyle signed off. She wished that she had something that she could slam down. Getting to her feet, there were too many questions that didn't have any answers. Looking at the door of the cabin holding the other Gunn, Boyle walked towards it. Punching in the code, she opened the door. The doppelgänger lay on the bed, not moving.

"Something is happening. I have spoken to mission control and it appears that things aren't as they should be," Boyle told her.

"I heard you."

"What have you done?" Boyle demanded. "Tell me!"

With a smirk, the doppelgänger taunted her. "You think that this was all caused by me? What about with the other Gunn? Can you be so sure that she is not the doppelgänger?"

"Don't bullshit me."

The doppelgänger laughed. Shuddering, Boyle watched as the other woman turned in the bed, allowing them to face each other. Neither of them spoke. Boyle tried to hide the disgust she felt at being close to this woman – this thing.

"What has the other Gunn seen? I know that something is happening," the doppelgänger hissed. "What is it."

"The stars are disappearing."

Turning, Boyle walked away. Looking back, the face of the doppelgänger appeared at the small, glass window that was set into the door, watching her as she walked away. Shuddering, Boyle felt grateful that there was no way to escape the cabin, once the door was locked.

"What's happened?" Gunn questioned.

"When I contacted mission control, a young man I have never seen before answered the video call. I asked him where Joe was, but no-one seems to know who I was talking about," Boyle told her. "It's as if he had never existed."

As Gunn turned to face Boyle, the lights flickered, before giving way to the dim emergency lights. Getting to the controls of the orbiter, Gunn swore to herself as she started to push buttons.

"What is it," Boyle asked.

"We've lost all main power," Gunn answered, without looking up from the controls. "We have enough emergency power to last until we get picked up. Let's just hope that those coming to get us are not late."

"And the doors of the sleeping cabins?"

Seeing Gunn's face fall, Boyle rushed off. In the darkness, she could make out that the door of the locked cabin lying open. Peering inside, she knew that she was too late.

Stumbling back the way she had come, Boyle shouted. "Gunn, she's managed to get out."

No answer. Slipping over to the communication area, she fumbled with a small compartment that was always kept locked. Feeling the cold metal of the gun at her fingertips, Boyle wished that she had another option. With a gasp, she quickly checked that the gun was loaded and flicked off the safety.

Boyle felt her way back to where she had left Gunn. Coming into the control part of the orbiter, a silhouette stood in the centre of the area.

"Boyle, she's hiding in the shadows. I don't know where she is," Gunn told her. "Where did you get that gun? I thought that we weren't armed."

Ignoring the question, Boyle hissed. "Which one are you?"

"You know that I'm Gunn," came the answer.

Nodding, thought for a moment. She had to be Gunn.

A cold laugh came out of the shadows. The other Gunn stepped out of the shadows, her arms stretched out on either side of her as she walked towards the other women.

"You know that one of us has to die," the other Gunn added. "Somehow we have created a paradox and that has to be corrected. It doesn't matter which one you chose - the result will be the same."

"Boyle, you know that I'm the real Gunn. We've been friends for years. She is right though. But, if anyone must die, kill the doppelgänger."

Hesitating, Boyle tried to hide the fact that her hands were shaking. She had never shot in anger. The firing range had been a place of safety. As her heart raced, Boyle felt what control she had slipping out of her fingers.

"Fuck it," the other Gunn shouted. "I will do it myself."

As the doppelgänger lunged at Gunn. Lashing out, all of Gunn's blows found their mark. Watching the blur of the two figures, Boyle tightened her grip on the gun. Raising it, she hesitated.

"Boyle, do it," one of the Gunn shouted.

The crack of the gun and the smell of cordite filled the air, as one of the Gunns slumped to the ground. In the shadows, Boyle gulped, glad not to see the damage that she had inflicted. The woman's breath rattled to a stop, with her accusatory gaze fixed on Boyle. Keeping her arms at her side, Boyle struggled to bring her breathing under control.

"What do we do now?" Boyle whispered.

"The space shuttle will be here soon, to take up back home," Gunn answered. "We will need to get rid of it before they show up."

"How do we do that? It's not like we can take her out somewhere and bury her?"

"Put her in the escape pod and send it to the surface. Ground control won't go after it. They will just replace it. We'll just have to make sure that they believe that it malfunctioned. We will tell them that it was released when we lost power," Gunn answered. "We cannot let anyone know that this has happened."

Boyle walked over to the porthole and looking out. The stars had stopped disappearing, but the ones that had already vanished had not returned. Dark patches of space were left, which had once been left with pinpricks of light.

Boyle walked through the corridors of mission control, with Gunn at her side. The knowledge that there was a body lying in the wreckage of an escape pod on Mars gnawed away at her. She did not want to think about what would be discovered when people first set foot on the surface of Mars.

Mission control was buzzing with excitement. Everyone wanted to see the returning heroes. They had been the first humans to have been that far away from Earth, and who had returned alive.

They were being led to the debriefing room by a young man. He had told them his name, but Boyle had forgotten it. All that she could remember, was that he was one of the psychologists, sent to evaluate them, while they were debriefed. The effects of being that far out into space, was ripe for exploration.

Neither Boyle or Gunn spoke, only glancing at each other. Seeing a look in Gunn's eyes, Boyle frowned and bit her lower lip, but could not bring herself to ask what she wanted to ask her friend.

With a twisted smile, Gunn walked off, without looking back. Trying to follow her, Boyle saw her friend disappear down one of the corridors, leaving nothing behind.

"Boyle, you have to come with me. You have to be debriefed about your mission," the young man stated. "There are some irregularities in the reports that you sent to us. We need to understand what happened while you were up in the *Mars Orbiter*."

Looking back to face him, she pointed to where Gunn had disappeared. "Gunn has gone off that way. She'll need to come with us."

"Gunn? Who's Gunn?"

"She's my colleague. She was up on the orbiter with me. She needs to be debriefed as well."

"Do you see Gunn now?" the young man asked.

"No," Boyle told him. "She disappeared down that corridor. She was about the same height as me, with red, curly hair."

Frowning, the young man took a couple of moments before he continued as if struggling to put his thoughts into words.

"There wasn't anyone up on the orbiter with you," he told her.

"Yes, there was. Gunn was up there with me for three months," Boyle hissed.

The young man took a step back, with his hand held up in front of him, in a gesture of reassurance. "There was no-one else up there with you. It was a solo mission."

The Slender Man

"Hello Detective Jerome," I sighed. "I know why you have come. In all honesty, I had thought that you would have been here, before now."

"Is that so?"

Nodding in reply, I watched him. He sat down on the other side of the table, facing me. There was a weariness in his eyes. That was the look of someone who had seen too much, too young and could do nothing about it.

I may have been watching him, but there were others who were keeping a closer eye on me. They always made sure that they kept themselves out of sight, but it didn't take much to realise that they were not willing to leave me unsupervised.

My wrists were cuffed and secured to the table in front of me. There wasn't a single person willing to trust me. There was no reason for them to trust me. I couldn't blame them. There was blood on my hands. Detective Jerome shuffled the paperwork in front of him, before continuing.

"As you will know, over the past few weeks, there has been a spate of disappearance. All of them have been children. We suspect that they have been murdered, but no remains have been found. It looks like we have a copycat on our hands," the detective told me.

Stopping, he looked up at me. With a sigh, he continued. "With the similarities between this case and your crimes, we need to talk to you about them. Given your history, you might be able to give us an insight into what is going on, and who might be behind these disappearances."

Shifting where I sat, I looked away from him. The interview room was bland, bare and windowless. There was nothing but the table and some chairs to fill it. It reminded me of the police dramas that my parents had watched when I was a child. That was another life, and long before my world was restricted to within the walls of the prison.

"These are not copycat disappearances," I assured him. "He's returned and we all know how this is going to play out."

The small suburban park was filled with shouts and laughter. Children chased each other and played their games. The adults looked on, smiling at the innocent happiness of childhood, while they gossiped about everything that had taken place over the past few days. The schools were out for the summer and the good weather was holding, proving to be better than any of the parents had hoped for.

No-one paid any attention to the woods that stood at the back of the play park. It was somewhere that the children were told to stay out of. No-one could give a reason for why the woods were dangerous. It had been that way for generations, and no-one questioned it.

As the afternoon crept closer to evening, parents and children started to drift off home. But, there was one mother who stood alone, looking for something that wasn't there.

"Nicola? Where are you?" she shouted. "Come on Nicola. Stop hiding. We have to head home."

Some of the other parents had stopped, glancing at each other. All of them watched, unsure of what they were do next.

One of the other mothers walked over to Nicola's mother. "Are you alright?"

"I can't find her. Nicola was playing here a moment ago, but she's disappeared. I need to find her," Nicola's mother sobbed.

I sat on the bench, on the side of the playpark, watching as others began to look for Nicola. That bench was my spot in the playpark, despite my mother's whispered pleas to play with the other children. I watched, while I remained unseen. The grown-ups believed that I was shy. All that I wanted to do, was to hide and have my nose buried in a book.

One of the parents was already on their phone. Looking away, I watched the others. Even at that age, I could see the fear and panic on the faces of the adults. I had seen the girl, as she walked over to the edges of the woods, but I hadn't seen where she had gone.

The sound of sirens filled the air, and the evening was filled with blue flashing lights. The police walked amongst us, asking everyone there what they had seen. Even then, I knew that Nicola would never be found. She had somehow gone from this world, with no trace of her being left behind.

With the agreement of the police, people made their way home, taking their children with them. All the children looked behind them, with their eyes being drawn to the treeline. I was the only child who didn't look back. I just couldn't bring myself to do so.

The days passed, and the town was quieter than it had ever been. All of the adults wanted to know what the police were doing? Why hadn't they found the missing girl?

Anger simmered, just below the surface. Everyone was expecting something to be done, yet, things were stagnating, despite the reassurances of the police.

The children, on the other hand, spoke of something else. Something much worse than what their parents were willing to accept. All of them whispered about the Slender Man. He was said to haunt the woods that edged the suburbs, and that he was patiently waiting for his next victim to wander into his domain.

During the day, gangs of children would prowl down to the woods, daring each other to go inside. They were to challenge the Slender Man to take them. With the coming of evening, they would run away, their screams quickly turned to laughter as they returned to their homes.

A week after Nicola disappeared, another child never returned home. Images of the missing child filled the evening news, only to be replaced by video footage of his weeping parents, as they pleaded for their son's safe return.

"No trace has been found of where either of the children have been taken, or what has happened to them," the news reader announced. "The police are advising parents to keep a close eye on their children, and to come forward if they have any information that could help with the investigation."

"It will be one of those paedophiles, I'm sure of it," my father stated, sneering at the very thought of it.

"Shhh, not in front of the kids," my mother told him. "They will be hearing enough bad things as it is, without hearing about that."

The news reader quickly moved onto happier stories, and everyone did their best to forget.

The playgrounds were empty. Parents were too scared to let their children out of their sight. That proved to be no defence. I had been watching the boy who lived next door to me through a hole in the fence. At school, he was the one that the girls fancied. I was trying to figure out why. The idea of attraction to someone else was proving to be something of an intriguing mystery that I wanted to understand.

He was playing keepie-ups, with a football. I blinked and he was gone, with the ball he had been playing with, rolling across the now empty garden.

Stepping back, I was not sure what I had just seen at first. Feeling a shiver running the length of my spine, I knew that he had been there. The Slender Man had been in my neighbour's back garden, brazen and confident that he would never be caught.

Slinking inside, I hid in my room.

I did not want to be outside when it was discovered that another child had disappeared. I didn't want to have to listen to the crying of others as the fear and panic began to spread again.

The weather was sweltering, and the children were being kept inside. Some whispered that there might be a serial killer, while the police remained closed lipped. Being kept off the street did not stop children from disappearing. The names of all of them were on everyone's lips – Nicola, Edward, Fiona and Paul.

I had been sitting at my bedroom window, watching as one of the other children on my street, walked out of her front door. He continued down the street in nothing, but his PJ's. His feet were bare, but he did not look as if he was aware of the stones that cut and scraped his skin.

Leaving my room, I walked into where my parents were sitting, watching evening television. "Mum, Dad. Nick from across the street is out. He's just walking down the street."

Walking across to the living room window, my mum peaked out from behind the net curtains. "Go back up to your bed and try to get to sleep."

"I'll go out and have a look. They can't have gotten that far," my dad added, as he pulled on his coat.

"Knock on doors and get others to help you," my mother told him. With a nod, my dad was out of the door as my mother got on the phone.

Going back up to my room, I hid under my duvet. The adults were wrong and they couldn't see that that they were wrong. Struggling to sleep, I knew that the Slender Man was out there. Drifting off into sleep, I slipped into the darkness of my dreams.

The forest was closing in around me, but I kept walking. There was not a single noise, not even from my feet, even as I kicked through the dead and dry leaves that littered the ground.

I wasn't alone. I could feel someone watching me, even though I could not see them. A voice finally cut through the silence, stopping me in my tracks.

"I want one blood sacrifice," the voice told me.

The coldness to those words made me shiver, as I continued to dream. Nothing more had to be said, I knew what I had to do, and nothing else would be good enough.

I had woken with a start. It was still early and I knew that everyone else would be asleep. Dressing quickly, I pulled on a long cardigan to keep off the chill that filled the house. Creeping into the kitchen, I pulled out a long, thin knife from one of the drawers. Slipping it into the belt of my trousers, the bottom of my cardigan comfortably covered it. No-one stirred as I walked outside and down the street.

Coming to the edge of the forest, I hunkered down, remaining out of sight. Paula appeared, walking towards where I was. She knew where to find me. We had organised it a few days before. Standing up, we nodded to each other.

"Are we really going through with this?" she asked, glancing at the shadow filled woodland.

I smiled. "Of course," I told her. "Don't tell me that you're scared. The others have been doing it."

Walking side by side, neither of us challenged the Slender Man to come and find us. Paula clung to my arm, yelping at even the slightest of noises. Keeping my eyes on what was before us, I swallowed the urge to run home and disappeared beneath my duvet.

Stopping in a clearing, I pulled out the knife as my mouth went dry. "We're not going any further."

As I turned Paula to face me, I saw the reflection of my knife in her widening eyes. Lifting it into the air, it plunged down, as if of its own accord, finding its mark with a practised ease that I certainly never had. She did not scream once as my attack continued. I wanted her to scream and to beg for her life, or at least to cry for her mother. Instead, I got nothing more than a stunned silence.

Voices shouted at me, as I stood over her body, my clothes and hands stained red. I can't remember hearing a single word that was said to me, as I was bundled away by two police officers, just the noise. Some of the parents from the town were starting to gather at the edge of the wood, wanting to know what was going on.

The only two who I did not see, were my own. Where my parents were, I was never told.

My memories of the trial are fleeting at best. The other missing children were presumed dead, and their deaths were quickly laid at my feet. I was sentenced accordingly. I know that I will never see the outside world again.

Life in an institution does have its perks. There is the clockwork routine, but none of the drudgery of the office jobs that others my age will have been forced to work, just to pay their bills.

There were those who claimed to be writers and journalists, who showed interest in my case and came to talk about what had happened. All of them want to be the one who will break my case. They all have the same plan – write books about what happened and make names for themselves. I guess that many of them leave disappointed when I never tell them what they need to hear.

My mother still comes to visit, but never my father. Separation and divorce came their way. The stress of what had happened proved too much for them. No-one knows that what I did was for the benefit for everyone. Until now.

It was one death to stop the suffering of others. A single blood sacrifice to satisfy the Slender Man. But I knew that it would only give the town a few years reprieve before his hunger again became too strong, and he returned.

"She was claiming that what happened twenty years ago was the actions of the Slender Man," Jerome reported to the rest of his team. "Apparently, he has returned and the only thing that will stop him will be a blood sacrifice."

"I remember hearing those stories when I was a kid. It was nothing but a stupid story to scare people with around a campfire," one of the others scoffed. "It sounds as if the looney bin is the best place for her."

"That may be the case, but we couldn't have taken the risk of not talking to her, just in case she had known something," Jerome replied.

Glancing at the clock that hung on the wall, it was the end of his shift. Leaving the police station, Jerome took the quickest way home. His wife had needed the car that day, so he was faced with the walk home. Walking through the suburbs, the path took him close to the woods. Stopping, he was sure that he had seen something move in the tree line. Peering into the shadows, he shook his head and made to move on, only to stop again, mid-step.

He had seen something.

There was someone standing there, keeping to the shadows. Whoever he was, he was tall, with legs and arms longer than Jerome had ever thought possible. The man in the tree line was dressed in black. Jerome would have sworn that the other man was staring right at him, but he couldn't make out their face.

Turning, he fled.

Running faster than he had ever run in his life, Jerome felt his lungs burning, begging for him to stop and catch his breath. Stopping in his tracks, he wanted to scream as the figure stood before him - but no sound came out. No matter how hard he fought it, he couldn't move. He felt his eyes widen, as the creature reached out for him.

A moment of pain filled Jerome. Then, there was nothing.

<u>Coldwell</u>

Parking the car in the dirt covered layby, Shan stepped out into the warm summer weather. She was only a few miles from the nearest city, yet, it felt as if she couldn't be further away. People rarely came this way, leaving her to her own devices. The air hummed with life and was scented with the smells of warm grass and fresh muck filled the air. Smiling, Shan couldn't help but reminisce on the endless summers of her childhood in the nearby village.

She strolled over to the locked metal gate. What she had come to see stood only a short distance away. Despite its closeness, it was hidden from the road. Even from where she was, she couldn't see it, but she knew that it was there. Coldwell House was waiting for her to explore it.

Climbing the gate, Shan kicked up dust when she jumped down onto the parched ground. Walking along the track, it took her a few moments to notice that the sounds of summer quietened as she got closer to the house. Looking up, she was greeted by the ruins, as they stood proud against the clear blue of the sky as if demanded her attention.

"Well, let's get this started," Shan whispered to herself.

Swinging her rucksack off her back, she rummaged through it, pulling out her camera. Snapping photos of the outside and headed around to the back. Underneath some trees, a rust covered children's playpark stood, neglected and unloved. Lowering her camera, Shan tilted her head.

There was something about this place. The walls were still standing, but the roof had been destroyed in a fire. The house was nothing but a shell, but hints of its former glory was still there. The windows were large, but now empty of any glass. Small trees were growing out of cracks in the house.

There was a creep factor. That was something that everyone spoke about, even the most sceptical of her friends found the place to be unnerving. Her friends had come up to Coldwell to explore the grounds and the outbuildings the previous summer.

There were cottages for those who had once worked the estate, along with ruined barns and stables – all in varying states of decay. Having been on holiday in the Costas, she had come back to the stories that they had to tell about the place.

Shan shook her head. "Don't be daft. You know that there's nothing wrong with this place. It's just abandoned."

Walking to the front of the house, she strode through where the door had once been. Standing there for a few moments, she could see the dilapidation of the inside. The roof, main staircase and the floors had long since been destroyed by fire. Holding her camera at the ready, she stepped inside.

Taking photographs as she walked, Shan smiled to herself. The others would be kicking themselves when she got back. Stopping, she frowned.

Something didn't feel right.

Shaking her head, she told herself that her eyes were just playing tricks on her. For a moment, it had looked that a shattered mirror had restored itself. Looking back at it, the mirror's glass was again in pieces, show many distorted reflections.

That explanation would have been fine if it hadn't happened again. This time, it didn't stop. The rubble and decay that filled the house were vanishing. It was like watching a demolition in reverse, with everything returning to where it had once been. Her head was spinning, and as it cleared, she found the house, as it had been in its hay-day.

"Oh, fuck this for a game of soldiers," Shan hissed, and turned on her heals.

Rushing to where she had walked in, Shan found the door intact and closed. Pulling at the handle, the door refused to budge. Shouting at it in frustration, Shan hit the flat of her free hand against the solid oak of the door.

Turning, she jogged through the house. She was certain that there had to be another way out. There had to be something, somewhere. Every door and window she tried were locked or jammed. Even trying to break the windows only saw the object she had thrown coming back at her, without leaving a scratch on any of the glass.

The house suddenly grew dark. Shan looked out a window. It was as if the sun had been eclipsed. Her jaw dropped She struggled to get the words out. "What ... what the fuck is happening here?"

Breaking out into a run, she fought against her legs, as they threatened to give way beneath her. Whatever way she turned, she always found herself running back into the main entrance hall. Pulling at the front door again, she hissed to herself when it remained shut.

"Please, don't go. You've just got here," a young voice pleaded from behind her.

Turning, and keeping the door firmly at her back, Shan felt her eyes widen at the sight of a young girl standing on the stairs. She was dressed as Shan had always imagined a young Victorian girl would be, with her hair curled to perfection.

"Who are you? Where did you come from?" Shan questioned, doing her best to stop her voice from shaking.

"I'm Jess," the girl answered, sweetly. "This is my home. Have you come to visit?"

"You can't live here. This place has been a ruin for decades. No-one has lived here since the fire, and that was before I was born," Shan answered, not wanting to accept what she was seeing.

"Coldwell is not a ruin. This is my home. I have other friends who live here, but I always like to make new friends," Jess smiled at Shan.

Coming down the stairs, Jess skipped over to Shan, the smile never leaving the girl's lips for a moment. Taking Shan's free hand, Jess giggled.

"What is that?" Jess asked.

"It's a camera," Shan told her.

"A camera? I saw one, once before. It was a lot bigger than the one that you have. Will you be taking my picture?"

Walking into the middle of the room, Jess posed. Taking a couple of shots, Shan put her camera back into her rucksack, before swinging her bag onto her back. She needed to get out. She needed to find a door that she could open.

"Is that it? I thought that it took longer than that to take photographs. Mother and Father used to have to sit still for an eternity, just to have theirs taken," Jess stated. "Did you actually take my photograph? Or were you only pretending?"

"It's a digital camera. They take photos really quickly. Is it okay if I can get out? It's time that I was heading home. My family will be looking for me, and I'm sure that they will be worried that I'm not back yet," Shan lied.

Jess looked at Shan, her eyes brimming with tears, and her hands pulling at the fabric of her dress. "Why do you want me to be lonely?"

Looking at the girl, Shan licked her dry lips. She could not be having this conversation. Ruins do not rebuild themselves, and little girls from over one hundred years ago do not demand that you take their photograph.

"I just need to get home. I'm supposed to be seeing my mum and dad. I just came here for a quick visit. That's all," Shan continued. "I'm sure that you parents will be wondering where you are."

"No, they don't," the girl smiled. "They left me here when they went to Heaven. Others come here and never leave. You will join them."

The girl flew forward, her hands out-stretched and clawed. Her face was no longer that of a little girl. Instead, it was twisted as the girl screamed like a banshee. Feeling the door swinging open, Shan rushed outside.

She could see her car a short distance away. If only she could get to it, she could make her escape, and drive away. She would never come back to Coldwell. Falling hard, she tried to crawl. There were only a few hundred yards to go.

She was nearly there.

She had to make it.

Feeling something grab hold of her ankles, Shan whimpered. For every centimetre she gained, she was dragged back two. Digging her fingers into the parched ground, she could feel the stones and gravel digging in underneath her fingernails.

As something cold forcing its way in from her back, Shan wanted to scream, but her voice froze in her throat. Long fingers of ice encircled her heart and slowly squeezed.

Stretching out her hand, one last time, Shan fought the darkness, as it encroached from the edge of her vision. Praying, she knew that no-one would listen. There was nothing there to help her.

Sitting up with a start, Shan looked up at the sky. The sun was high in the sky, and bathing everything in light, but the colours were muted. Shivering, she forced herself to stand up. Her car was still where she had left it, but it was now surrounded by people.

There were also people around her, all of whom were wearing uniforms. They were all police and paramedics. It took a moment before she realised that those at her car, were investigating it. What they were looking for, she had no idea.

"Hey," Shan shouted. "That's my car. Was I not meant to park it there?"

No-one turned to her or answered her question.

"I'm right here. Why are you not answering me? Can none of you hear me?" Shan asked, only to face the same reaction.

Walking to where her car was, she got as far as the gate, before something stopped her. She could go no further. Reaching out for the gate, she screamed as pain ripped through her. Dropping to her knees, she cradled her arm. Looking up through her tears, she watched as a team of paramedics walked towards her, carrying an empty stretcher.

They continued past her, only to stop at the spot where she had regained consciousness, Sniffing, Shan wanted to demand answers but knew that she would get none. There was something lying in the long grass, next to the track, right in front of where the paramedics had stopped. Whatever it was, it wasn't moving.

Getting back up, she walked over to them, uncertain if she wanted to see what it was. Stopping, she watched as they lifted the thing and placed it on the stretcher. It was nothing more than a husk that filled a body bag. The cold realisation that it had once been her sunk it. Now, she was unseen and unheard.

"It's a real shame. One of the police found a digital camera in her bag when they were trying to ID her. They looked at some of the photos, and it looks like she was a pretty good photographer," one of the paramedics stated, as they carried the body away.

"I'm just glad that I don't have the job of having to tell her parents," the other paramedic answered.

Once they had all driven away, Shan looked back at the house, now returned to its ruinous splendour. In the space where a window would have been, she could see the silhouette of a young girl, dressed in Victorian clothing. Shan now knew that the others tried to hide, but they were always found.

There would be no way for her to escape, and there was no-one to help her. She was the girl's plaything no. Nothing more.

The Man with Iron Teeth

The children of the Gorbals swarmed through the Southern Necropolis. All were armed with home-made tomahawks - ready to face the horror that they had all heard whispered. None of them wanted to go down, without a fight.

They had come prepared for the seven-foot-tall monster, iron teeth and all.

Some called him a vampire, who slept in the Necropolis in the day, and stalked the streets of the city at night.

Others had said that the Man with Iron Teeth had already killed and eaten two children. A friend of a friend had seen it happen.

The adults tried to shush the idea, all saying the same thing. No children had gone missing. No-one had been killed. If they had been, surely, they – the adults – would know about it.

The fad passed quickly, and no-one returned to the Necropolis. There was no need to hunt for vampires or monsters. The kids returned to the playgrounds that are the streets of the Gorbals.

But a shadow soon returned to the cemetery. All seven-foot of darkness and iron teeth.

Death Amongst Us

The statuesque blonde woman and her assistant continued to work on the corpse, which had been brought in that morning. A murder victim, which in the grand scheme of things, wasn't that uncommon. She had spent many years working in the city's mortuary, finding that she was more comfortable there. The mortuary was cold, clean and sterile; a place that was utterly under her control. It also helped that the dead did not ask any questions, or dare to answer back. Unlike the living.

She didn't have to be the goddess of death in order to realise that there was something different about this murder. She had been told about where he had been discovered, and his injuries were in keeping with that information, but the reasoning behind it wasn't proving to be so co-operative.

As with any murder case, there were two uniformed police officers standing at the door that led in and out of the mortuary. They were there to keep an eye on proceedings. A legal requirement in cases such as this. Looking up to the viewing gallery, she could see DC McBride looking down on what was going on below. A younger detective stood beside him, with the air of someone who was new to the role. Lowering her surgical mask, Hela walked over to the tannoy system and pressed the button that activated it, allowing her to speak with McBride and his companion.

"Good day, gentleman. I don't really need to ask if you are here in relation to the young man we are currently working on."

"You will have been brought up to speed," McBride commented.

"We have confirmed your assumption that this one was a local thug. His mother identified him. The only injuries that we can find are a series of small puncture wounds, like those found with snake bites. It is very likely that was the cause of death, but that still has to be proven beyond all reasonable doubt," she answered.

"That would fit with where we found him," McBride added.

"So, he was found in a pit with venomous snakes?"

McBride tilted his head to one side, before he continued. "He was. What are you thinking?"

"I know only of one other person who was killed by being thrown into a pit of venomous snakes."

"I've not heard anything about anyone else being killed like that," the young detective commented. "If you're wanting to kill someone, why not just use a knife?"

"You're new to all of this, aren't you?" she continued, giving him a cold look. "You won't have heard of the victim. Not unless you know anything of history."

"This is DC Mulligan," McBride told her. "Mulligan, this is Hela. She is the chief forensic pathologist."

Hela held Mulligan's gaze. He tried to hide the shiver that went down his spine. He felt as if she was looking right into his soul. He didn't have to be told to know that she was the sort who would be able to hold her own in most situations and he wasn't willing to get on the wrong side of her.

"Well then, DC Mulligan, legend claims that a Norse warrior and hero, Ragnar Lothbrok, was killed by one of the kings of England. As the story goes, he was thrown into a pit of venomous snakes. That was enough for the snakes to attack. Their venom caused him to die a slow and painful death. I suspect that the man before us did not have an easier time of it."

"So, we may have a killer on our hands, who has a thing for history and legends?" McBride questioned.

"The autopsy will have to be finished before I commit myself to saying anything. It may be obvious to us what the cause of death was, but we both know that we will need to make it official. I will have my report on your desk as soon as possible," Hela answered.

"I will look forward to reading it," McBride added. Hela watched them as they left the viewing gallery, leaving her to continue with her work.

Hela stood over the corpse. She had been taking notes as she worked, hoping that it wouldn't take too long for her to finish the task at hand. She had taken numerous tissue samples and they had been taken up the labs, and they had been taken to the lab to be processed, where it would be determined whether death had been caused by snake venom. The justice system was a stickler for all of the bases being covered.

As the autopsy was finished, all she was waiting for, was for the test results to come in. Once they had come back, Hela knew that it wouldn't take long for her to write up the report. It was late and she had sent her assistant on a coffee break. He wouldn't be back for twenty minutes. That would give her enough time to do what she needed to do.

Hela placed her hands on either side of the man's head and focused. She rarely did this, as the vast majority of deaths didn't warrant it. Most people died of natural causes, but there were things that only this man could tell her. With a sharp gasp from his lips, the dead man's eyes shot open.

"Where am I? What happened to me?"

"Listen to me. I need you to remain calm and to answer some questions. That is all that I ask," Hela told him.

He didn't answer, allowing for Hela to continue. "What can you remember?"

"I was out for a run when I got jumped from behind."

He stopped. Through the connection that they now shared, Hela could feel that he was struggling to remember what happened next, as well as how to put it all into words.

"I was knocked out. When I woke up, it was dark, but there was enough light for me to see that I was in some sort of pit. I could hear things moving close to me. It sounded like snakes. I could hear them hissing and slithering around."

"What happened next?" Hela asked.

His voice caught in his throat. "The snakes began to attack. I could feel them biting me. My body was on fire. There was nothing I could do. I couldn't get away. Oh my God, I'm dead!"

"Focus. Did you see the person who attacked you? Who killed you?"

Hela struggled to control her frustration, knowing that she only had a short time left to get information out of him. In his panic, she could feel him fight against her. There was still that part of him that wanted to run and hide, but his body was refusing to respond. She could feel him slipping away from her.

"I couldn't see him. I couldn't see him," he continued.

His voice was getting weaker as he spoke and his eyes fluttered shut as the connection deteriorated further. Hela knew that she had to let him go. She had more questions. There was only one thing that she could add to the investigation. Even though the victim hadn't seen his attackers face, he still knew enough to be able to say that the killer was male.

Hela let go of the cadaver and walked back to her desk and the paperwork. She continued where she had left off. Once her colleague returned from his coffee break, they placed the corpse into one of the chilled drawers. With nothing left to do, they both left.

"Good morning, McBride. I can see that you have brought me another cadaver. How many has that been in the past week?" Hela asked.

As before, McBride was standing in the viewing gallery, looking down at the mortuary. Even from that distance, Hela could see that there was a steely look in his eyes that he got when things were serious. She began to suspect that what she was going to see next was far from pleasant. Unlike his previous visit, McBride was standing alone.

"Where's your colleague?" she asked.

"In the nearest toilet, spilling his guts. We may need to harden him up a wee bit, when it comes to dealing with things like this, but I can't blame him for this one. I nearly lost my breakfast," McBride added.

Hela moved over to the mortuary slab, where the corpse had been laid and covered with a sheet. Removing the sheet, Hela could see why someone of McBride's experience would have such a reaction. The victim had been laid on his front, which was the only option that had been open to them, as he had been cut open from the back. What was meant to be inside was now on the outside.

"Who in their right mind would do that to someone?" McBride questioned.

"Someone who is really trying to make a point. This is a form of execution called a blood eagle. I am starting to think that we might be dealing with a serial killer, not just obsessed with history, but with the Vikings."

"What makes you think that the same person is responsible for these two murders?" McBride questioned. "It's not the same MO."

"With the first murder, the victim died after being put into a pit of snakes. As I said the other day, that was meant to have been how Ragnar Lothbrok died. That is not where the story ended. Once his sons found out, they were meant to have come to England, found the king who had murdered their father and killed him," Hela told him.

"And?"

"He was killed in pretty much the same fashion as we see here. His ribcage was opened from the back and his lungs pulled through the gaping hole that was created. Usually, this is done when the victim is still alive, but I will have to determine if that happened in this case."

Glancing at McBride, Hela thought that she could see a slight change in his expression. She wasn't sure what he was thinking. She was good at telling what was going through someone's mind, but Stephen was different. She struggled to read him much of the time. He was a hardened detective who had seen more than his fair share when it came to the worst of humanity. She had always presumed that he was doing nothing more than keeping his emotions under close raps, but there was a niggling feeling, at the back of her mind, that something wasn't as it should be.

"I'd better go and check on Mulligan. He seems to be taking his time," McBride commented. "Maybe, he's not wanting to come in and say hello."

Nodding, Hela turned her attention back to the corpse, there was much for her to be concerning herself with. The cause of death was obvious, but that did not mean that she didn't have her work set out for her.

Walking to where she had left her car, Hela understood why many of those who worked in the hospital hated the long journey to the staff car park. It never bothered her, even in the dark of night. She never felt threatened, but that did not mean that she was not aware of her surroundings. Her car was a short distance ahead, and she began to rummage in her bag for her keys.

At the same time, she got the niggling feeling that someone was close at hand and following her. Placing her other hand in the pocket of her long coat, she could feel the cool metallic canister of her pepper spray. She got to her car, but before she could get inside, a heavy hand grabbed her shoulder, forcing her forward against the body of the car.

"I hope that you are enjoying my presents," her attacker hissed. "I hope that you appreciate all of the effort that I am going to."

He was standing behind her, stopping her from going anywhere. Hela threw one of her elbows back and made contact with her attacker's torso, forcing him back, as he gasped for air. That was enough to give her all of the space that she needed. Spinning around, she took aim and sprayed the contents of her pepper spray into his masked face. With a cry, he staggered away.

"Are you sure that you're all right?" Mulligan asked. "You have had one hell of a fright. We certainly wouldn't blame you for taking a few days off."

As soon as the attacker had run off, she had called the police. She had expected McBride, yet it was Mulligan who had rushed over.

She may have been a goddess, but her powers and abilities did not protect her from everything that filled the Nine Realms. There was only so much that she could do, when it came to the living. Once they were dead, that was another matter.

"No, I'm fine. I will not let this bastard stop me," she hissed. "Are you here by yourself?"

"I called McBride when I heard about what happened, but he wasn't answering his phone. No one's been able to get a hold of him either. Don't ask me why," Mulligan told her. "Did you get a look at the guy who attacked you?"

"I didn't see his face, but I know that it was him. I know that he was our killer."

"How do you know? It could have been any nutter who was waiting for an opportunity to attack a woman who was out by herself."

"He referred to the two bodies that were brought into the morgue," she told him. "I know that neither of these deaths have been mentioned in the press. No-one involved in this has talked. So, the only people who know are us and the killer," Hela stated.

"Are you worried that he will come after you again? Are you wanting someone to stay with you?"

"No, I will be fine. You have other things to be dealing with. You don't need to babysit me. I should not have been stupid enough to walk into a carpark, by myself after dark," Hela told him.

"You've given your statement, so you don't need to stay any longer. Why don't you head home?"

With a weak smile, Hela got into her car. Closing and locking the doors, she started the engine and drove home. Pulling up outside the building where she lived, Hela studied the street. It was quiet and not a soul visible. Once she was inside her own flat and the door lock behind her, Hela relaxed. Someone was trying to take the power of life and death into their own hands. That was a power that they were never meant to have and she was not willing to standby and do nothing.

The sound of a phone ringing forced Hela to wake up quickly. It was early in the morning and it was still dark. Forcing herself to sit up, she answered the phone. For someone to call her at that time, it had to be something important and she didn't need to be told what the phone call would be about.

"Yes."

"Hela, it's McBride. I'm sorry that I wasn't able to help last night. There was something of a family incident that I had to deal with. Get down to the mortuary, ASAP. This sick bastard is not going to be stopping."

"I'm on my way."

It took her only a few minutes to get herself ready. She was soon out of the flat and in her car. The roads were quiet, allowing her to get to the mortuary quicker. Striding in through the front door of the lab building, she headed down the stairs, only to find McBride pacing along the corridor that led to the mortuary.

"Is it really that bad?" Hela questioned.

"That's the understatement of the century," McBride stated. "It appears that this poor bastard had his stomach ripped open and his intestines nailed to a tree. He ended up with his guts wrapped around the tree itself."

McBride walked away, heading towards the viewing gallery, allowing Hela to ready herself. Once she was fully kitted out, Hela walked over to the examination table where the corpse had been placed. Looking at what was left of him, it was clear that McBride's description hadn't missed the mark. Whoever this victim had been, when he was alive, he had been subjected to another ancient form of execution. He been forced to walk around the tree, tying himself to it. He would then have been left like that, to die slowly and alone.

"Is this what I think it is?" McBride asked, from the viewing gallery.

She didn't pay attention to him at first - she had been too absorbed with what she was doing. She had been shaken slightly the night before, but she was refusing to allow that to stop her from doing what she needed. No-one had gotten that close to her, with the intention of doing her harm. Not since she was a child and she was dragged from her mother's arm, only to be exiled to the world of the dead.

"What are your first thoughts?" McBride questioned her.

Finally answering him, Hela hissed. "I wish that I had stopped brought this all to an end last night."

"Leave that to us, just deal with what this piece of shit has decided to send up this time."

"Where's your partner? Is he in the toilet?" Hela asked.

"He phoned in sick this morning. He sounded rough" McBride told her. "Why do you ask?"

"I just wanted to thank him for helping me last night. I hope that he is feeling better soon."

"I'll pass the message on," McBride told her. "I will leave you to it then. You will have a lot to deal with and so do I. I'll speak to you soon."

McBride turned and marched out of the viewing gallery, leaving Hela to her work. There was something that he hadn't told her. There was more to this than ancient execution methods. Had she been sought out by the killer? Or was she reading too much into it? How much did he know about her? Had he chosen these methods of death out of a sick fascination with history, or was there really a message behind it all?

Now that she had time to think about it, there had been something familiar about the man she had seen the night before. She was sure that she had knew his voice, but it was clear that he had tried to disguise it. She hadn't been able to put her finger on it, but her thoughts on what had happened were beginning to clear.

Once the autopsy had been carried out, Hela quietly left the mortuary. There was someone she had to find, before anyone else ended up on her dissection table.

Hela hated seeing someone dying before their time. As she walked through the streets that surrounded the hospital, the city appeared to be devoid of all life. She slipped into the nearby park. Evening was already beginning to fall. The park was dark and silent, making it the perfect place for what she had in mind. No-one would see what was going to happen and that was the way that she wanted it.

People had always been warned about the dangers of setting foot within any of the city's parks after dark. That did not stop her. She could smell him. It was the familiar smell of someone who was meant to be upholding and protecting the law, but who had decided to take it into his own hands. The air was also filled with the metallic smell of blood. Another victim had been found and met their end.

Her eyesight was sharper than any mortals. This allowed her to see a figure, which was crouching in the shadows, partially hidden by the park's shrubbery. The killer. He was hard at work, unaware that he had been discovered. Hela moved towards him. He didn't notice her presence until she was standing over him. Reacting quickly, he grabbed at her, hoping to knock her off her feet. Grappling with him, Hela got her first glimpse of his face, confirming her suspicions.

Allowing herself to fall when he renewed his attack, Hela felt herself hit the ground hard. She could hear him laughing, as she pretended to have been hurt. He was taking his time, thinking that he had already won. He knew that she had seen his face, and had recognised him, but was certain that her death would stop her from telling what she knew.

"I wondered if you would figure this out," he laughed. "Mind you, I did try to make it difficult.

Those bastards deserved it, but I wanted to enjoy the game."

Getting to her feet, she looked McBride square in the face. "You give yourself too much credit."

As he moved towards her, Hela backed herself up against one of the nearby trees, but there was no fear in her eyes.

"Really?" he scoffed. "What makes you think that I care what you think?"

Hela could see the blade in his hand, still covered with fresh blood. He lifted the knife to her throat. Even in the dark, Hela could see the momentary look of disappointment. He had wanted to see her react, or to hear her scream. Instead, she continued to hold his gaze, defying him. His disappointment was replaced by anger as he began to press the blade into her skin.

Hela laughed, infuriating him further. She could feel the tingling of energy in her hands. Before he had the chance to cause any damage, she lifted her hands to his face, allowing the energy to flow through her. He tried to talk, but he only managed to babble incoherently. His muscles relaxed, forcing him to lose all control of his body.

Allowing him to fall to the ground, Hela watched McBride as he fought for breath. She could see the fear in his eyes as he struggled to understand what was happening. It slowly dawned on him, that there was nothing that he could do about what was happening. Hela crouched down next to him.

"How does it feel? Did you ever think that you would feel the terror that your victims had to face in their last moments?" she questioned, tilting her head to one side.

He couldn't speak, leaving it as a one-sided conversation.

"There is one thing that I never told you. It is easier if I show you."

Standing up, Hela drew herself up to her full height. The scales dropped from McBride's eyes, allowing him to see her for who she really was, showing her in all of her glory. The power that radiated out of her was enough to push McBride over the edge. She watched as his life slipped away. Hiding herself behind the mask that Midgard had come to know, Hela walked over to what was left of McBride's last victim.

It was Mulligan. There was nothing that could bring him back now, but she needed to know. Placing her hand on his head, she focused. The sound of a rattling gasp told her that it was time to ask her questions.

"Why did McBride attack you?"

"I found out what he was doing," Mulligan hissed. "He found out that I was going to tell our superiors and he needed to silence me."

"Why did he resort to murder? He had to have his reasons," Hela continued.

"He thought that criminals weren't being properly punished. He had become disillusioned with how things were. He was taking matters into his own hands," Mulligan told her.

"He has been stopped."

"I'm dead, aren't I?" Mulligan whispered.

"Yes. It's your time to go."

She could feel Mulligan slip away. She knew that he would find peace. McBride, on the other hand, would find his place in the darkest reaches off Helheim.

Walking back to the laboratory building, she took her mobile out of the pocket of her coat. Punching in the number, she was left an anonymous tipoff that something had taken place in the park near the hospital.

Hela sat in the hospital's café. She was eating by herself, not being one for spending time with others, unless she had to. Everyone in the labs had heard about what had happened in the early hours. All of them were struggling to come to terms with the knowledge that McBride had been behind the recent murders and that he was said to have committed suicide, after killing one of his colleagues. It wasn't just those who had known him. Even those who didn't know him could not understand how or why he could have carried out those terrible acts.

Someone came to a stop next to the table Hela was sitting at, breaking her train of thoughts. "How are you holding up?"

Looking up from her food, Hela found one of the lab assistants smiling at her. Smiling back, it was the only thing that she could do. Taking a moment, she thought about what she wanted to say.

"I'm holding up. As with everyone else, I'm shocked by what has happened," Hela answered. "It just reminds us that we should always expect the unexpected and never to take things for granted."

The young woman gave a shy smile, and made an excuse, before going on her way. Turning her attention back to her lunch, Hela allowed her mind to wonder, until another presence pulled her back. Looking up, Loki stood next to her table, looking down at her. It was clear that the others already knew.

"Father. What can I do for you?"

"Am I not allowed to come and visit my daughter?" he asked, sitting down at the table.

"You only come to visit when you want something," she answered, with a slight frown.

He laughed. She watched him closely. He was dressed in faded jeans, a t-shirt featuring the logo of some long-forgotten rock band, which was topped off by a tattered leather jacket. As always, he could not keep still.

"To be honest, I thought that it would have been the All-Father who would have shown up," Hela continued.

"Well, he's kind of busy at the moment. If I'm not mistaken, he is dealing with something in Iceland. Something that he wasn't even willing to tell me about," Loki told her. "So, did you manage to sort out what happened here?"

"Yes."

"Is that all you're going to say on the matter?"

"Well, the man is now dead. He has gone to the grave with what he knew," Hela told him, sharply.

Nodding, he got up. After one last look, he walked towards the exit of the hospital. Watching him go, Hela wondered when they would see each other again.

She wasn't the sort for sentiment, as she had become used to her own company. But the others were still out there. That was enough to stop her from feeling completely alone. Soon, her father was out of sight. Getting up, she made her way back to the mortuary and to the work that was waiting for her.

He Will Come from the Shadows

"He will come from the shadows."

That is what my grandfather said with his final breath. That was after he whispered that innocent blood was on his hands.

Who this man was and what he had done, my grandfather never said. His breath rattled in his lungs and his life fled from him, before he had the chance to say.

I am now sitting here, in the darkness. Waiting.

I know that he is coming. Looking up, I can see him stepping out in front of me. I can't see his eyes, but I know he has come for me.

Past Bound

Dr Saga Burke sat at her desk in the corner of her office. Every available wall space was covered with shelves, filled with more books than she cared to count. Being surrounded by so much history made her feel at home. She had *lived* through much of it, but seeing how events were remembered always fascinated her.

She had spent many years working within academia. It had meant moving from university to university and using different names, but that was the way of it. It was the same for all her siblings, those that hid in plain view.

She turned her thoughts back to the task at hand, the end of term papers. Focusing, she marked as many papers as she could. She looked up at the clock; it was getting late. A glance at the room's single window confirmed the time, as it was already dark outside. She got to her feet and pulled on her long winter coat and made ready to leave.

Before she got to the end of the corridor, a young man appeared from one of the other offices. Alasdair Sinclair's nose was buried in a book on medieval Scandinavia. Saga smiled. He was a post-doctorate who specialised in the history and culture of Northern Europe. Glancing up from his book, he started, clearly unaware that anyone else had been close by.

"I'm sorry. I didn't mean to give you a fright," Saga said.

"That's all right. Been working late again, Dr Burke?"

Closing his book, he stowed it away in a knapsack. Alasdair was young, with short strawberry blonde hair. Saga wondered if he was ready for the cut-throat world of academia, but he worked hard and it was clear he wanted to prove himself. Since his arrival in the department, a few months before, he had become a popular member of staff.

"Call me Saga. There's no reason to be overly formal," she replied. "I can see that you've been burning the midnight oil too."

"Too much work, not enough time," Alasdair answered as they continued towards the exit.

Saga allowed Alasdair to open the door for her. "It doesn't get any easier. Trust me, but I'm sure you will do brilliantly."

"Thank you for the vote of confidence," he replied, with a warm smile.

Once outside, they went their separate ways. Saga had a quiet evening to look forward to. It was certainly a far cry from her former life, when she had been one of the All-Father's closest confidants.

But that life was gone.

She rarely had any contact with any of the others. It wasn't as if she was trying to keep the others at arms-length, she just preferred the peace and quiet that her mundane life offered her.

No mortal ever knew of who they really were. The All-Father had made it clear to them all, that the consequences of anyone finding out would be dire. Both for them and the mortals. Humans were like children. They needed guidance, but they had a tendency to destroy anything they did not understand. That was how it had been for countless centuries and it looked as if that was how it was going to stay.

Alasdair's office was small, little more than a broom cupboard. But it was still his own space. It was where he could do his research. The idea of having to teach still made him nervous. A small part of him felt he would not do justice to those who had gone before.

He sighed, stretching. He needed to clear his head. Time for fresh air and lunch. Stepping out of his office, he spotted a familiar figure a short distance away.

Saga was struggling with the vending machine. As far as Alasdair was concerned, its coffee was not fit for human consumption.

"Saga, I don't think that's been working since yesterday. Someone was meant to come out. I'm guessing that they can't have been yet," Alasdair commented.

"That's just my luck. It always seems to break when I want to use it," she laughed. "I must be jinxed."

"I'm just heading out for lunch. Why don't you join me?" he asked. "I'm sure that a break would do you good. Plus, you could get some proper coffee."

Glancing at him, a slight smile crossed her lips.

"Know what, I think that you might be right. You can tell me all about your research over lunch."

"Well, if you're interested in hearing about the history of slaves in Norse Dublin. I know just the place."

Leading her out of the department and through the side streets of Glasgow's West End, he had a specific place in mind. He had spoken with Saga on a few occasions. Their conversations had always been comfortable, but she made him feel like he was stepping into the unknown.

He glanced at her, then quickly looked away, a slight smile tugging at his cheeks.

Saga watched Alasdair as he worked. He was sitting at the desk in her apartment, muttering to himself as he tapped one fingered at his laptop's keyboard.

She had taken a number of lovers in her life, but none of them had proved to be as passionate, so willing to please, as Alasdair. They spent more and more time in each other's company.

There were always going to be aspects of her life that he was never going to know. None of her former paramours had ever discovered the truth and it was going to stay that way. That didn't mean that she didn't care for Alasdair, but the end of their relationship was inevitable.

That only made Saga determined to enjoy what time she had with him. They had been together for a few months, but had managed to keep it quiet in the hope of avoiding office gossip. Despite their efforts, it didn't take long for rumours to start doing the rounds.

Letting out a sigh, Alasdair rubbed his eyes. Saga walked up behind him and gently massaged his shoulders. He began to relax as she continued to work the knots out of his shoulders.

"Are you all right?" she asked.

Alasdair looked up and gave her a smile. "It's nothing important. I know what I'm meant to be writing, but I'm struggling to find the right words. How am I going to be able to get that promotion, if I can't even write a decent research paper?"

"Maybe you need a break. You've been working hard," Saga answered. "I have an idea for something that might help."

"What?" Alasdair asked, cocking his eyebrow.

Getting him to his feet, she guided him back to the sofa. Both of them sat down, facing each other. A look of curiosity flitted across Alasdair's face, though he remained silent. He watched her closely, as if hoping to figure out what she was going to do next as she lifted her hands to the side of his face.

"You'll have to trust me. Close your eyes and breathe deeply. This is nothing more than a relaxation technique."

Smiling again, he did as she asked. As he took slow, deep breaths, Saga closed her own eyes and focused her thoughts. She could feel the familiar tingle of energy as it passed through her. She channelled it into Alasdair. She had done this for others, when they needed inspiration. It had often proven successful. The list of her lovers included some of the most famous of all writers and poets, none of whom realised how the seeds of their greatest works had been planted.

Opening her eyes, she watched Alasdair's face. The shadow of a smile crossed his lips as he sank into the sofa. Feeling that her work was done, Saga eased Alasdair back into the here and now. Opening his eyes, he sprung to his feet, before pacing, excitedly.

Saga smiled. "It helped?"

"I have no idea what you did, but it more than helped," Alasdair answered. "It's as if whatever was stopping me from writing is no longer there. I could almost visualise the lives of those slaves. It was as if I was there. What would I do without you?"

Saga strolled into the department. She hadn't seen Alasdair for a week, but that did not worry her. She collected her mail then continued onto her office. This was her quiet day. No lectures, or meetings. Peace and quiet was all that she needed to be getting on with her work.

She dumped the mail on her desk. There was one that stood out. There was no address, stamp or postmark – just her name scrawled across the envelope in a handwriting that she recognised straight away. It was Alasdair's.

She opened it.

I need to speak with you. It is urgent! I will be waiting for you in our usual coffee shop at Ten O'clock.

Reading it again, Saga frowned as she fished her mobile from her bag. She had better get going if she was going to make the rendezvous.

Alasdair was already sitting at their usual table, nursing a coffee. Saga smiled at the girl behind the counter and ordered. Then she took her drink and she sat down next to Alasdair.

"What is it that you are not telling me?" Alasdair demanded.

Laughing lightly, Saga smiled. "I don't know what you're talking about? I've not been hiding anything from you."

"Yes, you have. Tell me."

"Alasdair, what are you going on about? You're starting to worry me."

Watching him as he took another sip from his coffee, Saga covered his free hand with her own. He didn't pull away, but the warmth that she had once found there was missing.

"Don't make this any more difficult than it is all ready," he whispered.

"I don't know what it is that I am meant to have done. What has changed?"

"It all started when you did that relaxation technique on me," Alasdair continued. "I keep catching glimpses of things that I shouldn't. Things that no-one alive could know."

"Oh? That's unusual."

"It all started when you did that relaxation technique on me," Alasdair continued. "I kept catching glimpses of things than I shouldn't. Things that no-one alive could know."

"Oh? That's unusual."

"You think?" He stopped and stared out of the window for a moment. Taking a deep breath, he looked back at her.

"It was all great for the first couple of days. Everything was flowing and I was writing my best work. That was until I began to know things. I would catch glimpses as I walked past places. I saw people who shouldn't have been there – people who I knew were dead."

Alasdair held her gaze.

"Maybe you have been working too hard," Saga told him. "I think that you should see someone about this. It can't be right that you're seeing things that aren't there."

"I am not losing my mind. I know what has been going on. I don't know how I know it, but I know what you are. It's connected to what happened last week."

Saga cocked her head to one side and regarded him coolly. She had been so certain that she had been careful. Finishing off her coffee, she waited for Alasdair to continue.

"You're not human. Are you?"

Getting to her feet, Saga looked down at him. "I don't have time for this."

Walking out, she knew that this was not the end of the matter. She took an alley, hoping to get away from Alasdair, but he followed. Saga turned. She regretted what was going to have to happen.

"You're one of the Norse goddesses, aren't you? I am presuming that the others are about somewhere," Alasdair whispered. "If you are wanting me to keep quiet about who you are and what you can do, you'll ….."

"I will what?" Saga demanded, her voice edged and sharp.

"You'll help me get my professorship. Yeah, you get me tenure," Alasdair smiled. "If you don't, I will do everything that I can to expose you and your kind to the entire world."

Saga held his gaze, until he turned and walked away. A sudden caw caused her to look up. Two ravens perched on a nearby lamp-post, watching her with twinkling black eyes. She nodded in resignation. She knew what it was that she was to do.

Saga entered the darkened library. It was night, but that did not mean closed. Just the flash of her staff card was enough to get her inside. Walking through the darkened halls, there was a small number of students doing all-nighter.

There would be no-one working where she was going, though Alasdair would be waiting. As before, she had received a note. It was nothing more than a statement of where and when they would meet.

At least they would not be overheard. Sighing to herself, she reigned in her feelings as she took hold of the door handle. This would be the last time she got embroiled emotionally with a mortal. The next time, it would be different.

Walking into the room, she saw her lover, quickly making eye contact with Alasdair.

"I knew that you would come," he said.

"There is a lot that has to be discussed."

"That's true," he smiled. "Shall we start?"

"I wasn't meaning between the two of us."

"What are you on about?" Alasdair demanded.

They were not alone after all. She had felt the presence the minute that she had walked in. Alasdair followed her gaze as a familiar figure stepped out of the darkness. His wide brimmed, grey hat was pulled down over where his missing eye. Stumbling back, Alasdair steadied himself against a nearby table.

"Who the fuck are you? How the hell did you get in here?" he hissed.

"Hello Alasdair," the All-Father growled. "How I got in here is none of your concern, but there is much for us to discuss." He strode closer to the mortal, lifting the patch covering his eye.

And Death Took a Holiday

No-one wants to die. Yet, no-one wants to grow old. As poor old Echo discovered to her detriment, eternal life does not mean eternal youth. She should have been more careful about what she had asked for. Proper and clear syntax is that important.

Let me tell you of the time Death took a holiday. At first, no-one noticed that something was wrong.

The habit of reading the daily obituaries had long since fallen out of fashion. No-one paid any real attention to the deaths of others, unless someone famous shook off this mortal coil in some drug-fuelled binge, or with a smile on their face.

At first, it did not appear particularly strange that people weren't dropping down dead. After a week, the continuation of life started to be commented upon. It was discussed and debated in pubs, shops, and finally, in the gilded halls of Parliament. Experts were asked, but no answers were given. All that they could offer were a series of confused suggestions.

People in hospitals, who had been given hours to live, were still holding on, weeks later. Yet none of them were getting no closer to crossing over to the other side. They just weren't getting better. All that they could do, was to remain and patiently wait for Death, only to find that he was late in paying them a visit.

Business for funeral directors began to dry up. No new cadavers came through their doors. There was no-one to bury, and there certainly wasn't anyone to cremate. Many started to consider new, more lucrative lines of work.

Time began to creep by, relentless and unforgiving. Babies were still being born and people continued to grow old. As their bodies began to fall apart, life refused to give them up. The whispers of fear creep across the globe. No-one could die.

People had tried, only to be left mangled, yet still in the world of the living.

A dark figure finally came back to Earth – happy and relaxed from a much-needed holiday. Underneath his hood, he smiled at the thought of getting back to business. There were deaths to be taken care of, and the list certainly wasn't getting any shorter.

Striding into the hospital, list in hand, Death found the first name that had been scrawled on it. Standing over the person in question, a single touch was all that was needed to get the ball rolling. Ignoring the beeping's of the machines, as that one life came to its end, Death walked through the swarming mass of doctors. There were plenty of other who had waited long enough for a visit.

<u>The Night Mare</u>

It was the sound of the neighbour's dog barking that dragged her out of sleep. It slept in its owner's yard, finding little shelter in the tumble-down dog house that had been built for it years before. That dog woke her every night – always at the same time.

Something wasn't right. Dismissing it as being a trick of her tired mind, the young woman tried to sit up.

Nothing happened. Blinking, she was certain that she was awake, yet her body remained rigid, unmoving and unwilling to co-operate.

The dog had stopped barking. The light creaking of a floorboard caught her attention. Straining her eyes, which was the only part of her body that she could move, she saw nothing at first, only shadows.

Blinking again, she tried to tell herself that one of the shadows couldn't have just moved. That was until it moved again. She wanted to shout for help, as a wizened, ancient figure emerged, dressed in rags and dirt shuffled towards her. No matter how much she wanted to shout and scream, no sound escaped from her paralysed vocal cords.

All she could do was to watch, as the hag pulled herself up onto the bed. The young woman could feel the bed dip and move as the hag crawled into position. The hag dug into the bed clothes with the dirty, claw tipped fingers of one hand, while

78

caressing her victim's cool skin with the withered remains of her free hand. The hag's knees dug into the young woman's chest, as the reek of death enveloped her.

The young woman, hoped and prayed that help would come. She could feel the pressure on her chest, as it forced the air out of her by the weight of the hag. The young woman could see the hag, peering down at her. Waiting, waiting, waiting, as she read the young woman's soul.

There was someone else there. The young woman couldn't see them, but they were there. She could hear them breathing. Whoever they were, they were right next to her, breathing into her ear.

"We feed on your fear," the unseen figure whispered into her ear. "We will come again. Your fear keeps us strong."

With a start, she sat up.

The room was empty. There was no-one else there. Expecting silence, the still night air was filled with the sound of the neighbour's dog barking. Getting to her feet, she slipped across to the bedroom window. Peeking out from behind the curtain, the street was still. The dog barks filled the air, he remained out of sight, hidden and ignored by everyone.

As if on cue, the dog gave one final bark. His nightly duties had come to an end.

Going back to the warmth of her bed, the young woman curled up, dismissing all that she had seen as nothing more than a waking dream. A trick of the brain. Scary at the time, but nothing to be worried about.

79

Two haggard figures stood across the street, keeping to the shadows, as they watched and waited. Fading into the darkness, they would return soon enough.

Past Trauma

The machine shuddered, promising to spring into life, only to shudder to a stop, as if unwilling to fulfil its one, simple task. Growling to herself, Anya slumped onto the beat-up sofa that had been pushed up against the wall of her workshop.

Glancing around at her surroundings, all she could see was the remains of projects, all in various stages of completion. The creation of mechanical objects was the only things that took her mind off the fear that had stalked her since childhood. Never leaving the house that had once belonged to her parents, Anya lived on food that was delivered by a man she never saw.

He left the bags on the doorstep and would take the money hidden under the upturned plant pot. Even going that short distance, just to hide the money, Anya would feel herself coming out in cold sweats. Her eyes would dart from one thing to the next, finding danger hidden everywhere. With her panic building, she would scuttle back into the safety of her tumble-down home.

Paint was peeling from the walls, while the carpets needed to be replaced. The furniture was past dated, but Anya didn't care. It was her home. Within its walls, she was safe. That was until a few days before, when things started to go wrong.

She was certain that there was someone tampering with her work. Machines that had been working perfectly for her the day before, were now refusing to do what they were meant to do. Every morning, she had to get up and fixed what had gone wrong. Only then, was she able to make any progress, which was again undone by the next morning.

She just could not figure out how they were doing it. Only she had the key to get into her home. There was also the issue that she was the only one who knew how to work the alarm system for the house. She could have sworn that they were focusing their attention on her main project – the time machine.

Despite what many would like to believe, the time machine was a simple enough. It was nothing more than a metal box that was large enough for one person to get inside it. Once inside, one wall was filled with a control panel. With the correct information, they could travel to any point in the past. She only had one date in mind.

Getting back on her feet, she paced back to the time machine.

Placing her hand on its metal surface, Anya remembered the day when it had all started, only for the image of the crazed lady to fill her thoughts. The woman had appeared from nowhere – her hair wild and unkempt. Whoever she had been, she had grabbed Anya, her fingers digging into Anya's arms. The woman had shouted that she needed to run, and get away from danger.

Picking up her tools, she continued to tinker. All that she had to do, was to stop that crazed old woman and get her younger self to safety. History would rewrite itself, giving her the life that she deserved.

"Yes!" she hissed as the machine shuddered into life and continued to work. Stepping back, she smiled to herself, admiring the thing of beauty that she had brought into the world.

Walking into the machine, Anya punched in the information that she needed. Pausing, she recalled the date. Entering that information, it took a moment before she realised what was taking place. The world spun around her. Holding on tight, Anya closed her eyes and prayed to a god that she didn't believe in.

As everything shuddered to a stop, she opened her eyes and peered out into the world beyond. It was as she remembered it. Staggering out into the park, the sunlight hurt her eyes. Lifting a hand to shield them from the glare, allowing her to scan the park, while the machine remained hidden amongst the shrubbery.

She wanted to run and hide. She wanted to be back home, where no-one could possibly hurt her. Fighting back her panic, this one simple thing would break the cycle that had destroyed her old life. This one simple change would take away her fear.

Anya stepped forward, but kept to the treeline. She could see the play park. She could see her younger self playing, without a care in the world. That was where it had all started, and where her life had been brought to a sudden halt. Looking around, there was something missing.

"Where is she?" Anya whispered to herself. "Where is that evil old bitch."

Not giving it a second thought, she rushed forward. She had to act. Even though her stomach knotted with fear, there was not time to lose. Seeing her younger self, she jumped the fence and grabbed the child she had once been by the shoulders. Her younger self needed to know. She had to get herself to safety.

"Listen to me," Anya shouted at her younger self. "You have to get out of here. You have to run. Go home. Don't look back. Promise me that you won't look back."

"Get off me. Get away from me," the young Anya yelled, tears streamed down her face. "Daddy. Daddy, she's hurting me."

The cold realisation dawned on her. Letting go of the child Anya, she didn't even see the child run away. Could it have been that way all along? It was all clear to her now.

Painfully clear.

Someone shouted, snapping her train of thought. Looking up, she was greeted by the sight of her father marching towards her. At first, she wanted to run to him. Seeing him alive was enough to make Anya smile.

The feeling of joy quickly disappeared when she heard what he was shouting. He did not know who she was. All he saw was a threat to his little girl. Turning, she fled, stumbling through the shrubbery. Stopping next to the machine, she stared at it.

Looking at her reflection in the polished metal, she sobbed at what she saw. A crazed woman, her hair wild and unkempt. Pulling herself into the machine, she punched in the details. A new plan was beginning to form. There was only one true way to correct what had happened.

This time, she would not fail.

<u>The Ravens Have Flown</u>

The Tower of London was dark.

That early in the morning, it was always filled with shadows, as the early morning light had yet to creep over the Tower's ancient outer walls. That did not stop the ravens from needing their breakfast.

Feeding the birds fell to Gillian, warder of the Tower and Ravens Master. That morning, it was going to be biscuits soaked in blood. It was a firm favourite of the ravens, and she certainly did not want to disappoint.

Having served in Afghanistan, South Africa and India, Gillian had been more than willing to accept the offer of yeoman warder of the Tower of London. Only those who Victoria, the Queen and Empress, deemed worthy, received such an invitation. Few were ever chosen, and it was a job for life. Having been the first woman to become yeoman warder, there were those who had frowned and disapproved, only to be proven wrong.

She expected to hear the ravens squawking and calling to each other, waiting for her. Instead, she was greeted by silence. The ravens were never that quiet. That was enough to make her catch her breath and to quicken her pace.

Biting her lip Gillian on as she tried to ignore her worries. She told herself that the quietness was nothing more than the ravens being up to their old tricks. They were clever birds, and Gillian was certain that they were more intelligent than some people she knew.

The other warders of the Tower did all that they could to avoid the ravens, believing them to be ill omens. But everyone knew the legend, and no-one was willing to take the risk of facing the consequences.

It had been whispered for centuries, that if the ravens were ever to leave the tower, the Tower would crumble and the realm would fall. That was enough for the ravens to be kept in the Tower and for a Ravens Master to be employed. Being the only one not scared of the ravens, Gillian had taken her role of Ravens Master seriously from day one.

Entering the quadrangle, where the ravens were kept, Gillian froze. In the low light, she could see the raven's cages were all open and overturned. There was no sign of the ravens. None of them called out at the sight of her. Dropping the bucket of food, she rushed over, checking what little was left, only to find nothing but wrecked cages.

The ravens had to have flown.

Lifting the small steel whistle that she carried, Gillian gave a single, sharp blast. Figures began to appear from the surrounding buildings, some ready for the day, while others were in varying stages of undress. Every single one of them was armed, ready for all and every attack. Some of them carried batons, while others carried riffles. Some even carried swords.

Looks of confusion crossed their faces, once they realised that they were not under attack. Instinct forced them to remain at the ready.

Everyone stood to attention as the last figure entered the quadrangle. Chief Warder McKenna had come to see what commotion was about. As he waddled over to Gillian, his face was set.

"What is the meaning of this, Ravens Master?" he demanded.

"It's the ravens, sir," she stated. "There's no sign of them, and their cages have been destroyed. They know when I come to feed them and they are always waiting for me. There is not sign of them, but they would not leave of their own accord."

Quickly studying the carnage, McKenna motioned to the others. "Go on then. Find out where these bloody birds have gotten to. You will wait here, with me, Ravens Master."

Remaining rooted to the spot, she watched as everyone else disappeared, carrying out their orders and leaving her alone with McKenna. The other warders may fear the ravens, but they feared the consequences of their loss more.

Refusing to fidget, Gillian remained silent, waiting until she was spoken to. McKenna stood, waiting, unflinching, as the others began to return.

"Sir, there's no sign of the ravens," one of the others panted, after running back into the quadrangle.

Hissing to himself, McKenna paced.

"A clear act of terror on the state of Great Britain. Eastern zealots, the Indian Freedom Movement, the

Caledonian Rebels. It could have been any of them," he muttered to himself.

"Sir, orders?" one of the men asked, shaking the McKenna from his thoughts.

"Yes," he thought for a moment. "Word needs to be sent to the Palace. Her Imperial Majesty must be protected. You," pointing at one of the men. "Come with me. The rest of you will remain here. No-one is to find out about what has happened here. The Tower must continue as normal. Nothing is to be said of this, to anyone."

Gillian continued with what duties she could. Every time she glanced at the skies, she expecting to see the ravens returning to roost. The Tower was too quiet without their squawked conversations. The wreckage of twisted metal and shattered wood that had once been their cages had been removed. It would take time before they were replaced.

With the ending of her shift, Gillian returned to her quarters. They were plain, but homely. Nick knacks filled every available space in her quarters. Every piece bought back memories of good times, as well as sad times. There were artefacts of war, as well as of the civilian life that she had long since left behind.

Fished out what few civilian clothes she still had from the bottom of an old tea chest. They were simple enough, nothing more than breeks and braces, with a white shirt. It was all topped off with a warm overcoat. Pulling on a flat cap, she slipped out beyond the Towers walls, and into the streets of the London.

Walking on, she kept her hands buried deep in the pockets of her coat, and the collar turned up. Gillian knew that someone was following her through the London fog. It was nothing more than the tingling feeling in the back of her neck, warning her to be on her guard. Ducking into the nearest pub, strode across the sawdust covered floor. Nodding to the barkeep, she took her place amongst the other drinkers.

The barkeep had run that pub for longer than anyone cared to remember. He knew everyone in the area, listening to everything that was discussed within his pub, waiting to impart what he knew to the right customer. For the right price, of course.

"What will it be then? The usual pint of piss?" the bartender winked.

"I've always wondered how you can be a barkeep and not appreciate the glory of stout," Gillian retorted, lightly.

"You know fine well that I'm an ale man, through and through," the barkeep continued, pouring Gillian her pint.

Taking it from him, Gillian gulped down half of the glass, before placing it down on the bar.

"Careful girl," the bartender commented. "I know that you army types could drink the rest of us under the table, but I don't really want to see you drinking me dry before the night's out."

"Don't be giving me any ideas," Gillian winked back. "I might just try that."

Watching the others in the bar, none of them showed her any interest. They all knew her and left her alone, but the feeling of being watched was still there. Nodding to the barkeep, she waited until he had walked back over to her before she said anything to him.

Leaning forward, she kept her voice low. "Don't be giving yourself away, but is there anyone behind me, looking shifty, or out of place? Anyone who might be watching me?"

Leaning on the bar, the barkeep cleaned a pint glass. "Well, you know what this part of London's like. It has always verged on the seedy. There are a lot of shady characters who like to call this place their local. I don't pay them much mind. I just take their money and facilitate the only enjoyment that they might have in their shitty little lives. But since it's you...."

His gaze quickly swept across everyone in his establishment with an ease that rarely gave him away. He kept talking, saying everything and nothing. He had the practised art distraction that was only found in the barkeeps of London's less affluent establishments.

They were the skills of someone used to keeping trouble from his door. All without refusing money from willing customers.

Looking back at Gillian, he nodded, knowing that he would not be overheard. The others who surrounded them were too addled with drink to remember anything more than a blur.

The barkeep continued to clean the same pint glass. "There is one. A young man, who is giving himself away too easily for my liking. He is watching you like you are some sort of prize. If you are going to be teaching him a lesson, be kind enough to take it outside. Then you're not my problem."

"What does he look like?"

"He's a small, weasely thing – a slimy little maggot of a man that I've ever seen."

Paying for her pint, Gillian downed what was left of it, before marching outside. Doing so, she eyeballed the only man who could be the one the barkeep had described. The challenge had been accepted. Stepping outside, she ignored the puddles that were left over by a passing shower

The streets were filled with the din of steam cars and horse drawn carts. Feeling the reassuring weight of her standard issue pistol in the pocket of her overcoat, Gillian kept walking. Stopping at a corner, she stepped into the mouth of the alley and leant against the wall. All that she had to do now, was to wait for the young man who had been watching her. It didn't take him long to make an appearance.

As he came to a sudden stop, she made the first move. "What is it that you have to say to me?"

Looking one way and then the other, he walked over to her. "You're the Ravens Master, aren't you?"

Nodding, Gillian waited for him to continue. He may not have been an assassin, but what he was, she was still trying to figure out.

Stammering, he kept his voice low. "Your ravens. They weren't taken by any human."

With the cock of an eyebrow, Gillian folded her arms in front of her.

"Why am I not surprised that you are one of those conspiracy idiots?" Gillian laughed. "Have you been reading too many penny dreadfuls?"

"Not so loud," he hissed.

"So, who took my ravens?"

"Monsters," he whispered. "Dreadful, unnameable things that no person would want to see. It was them who freed your ravens."

With a cold look and a sigh, Gillian struggled to hide her disdain. "Alright, humour me. Please tell me, why would monsters want to remove the ravens from the Tower?"

"They know of the legend. Everyone does. They know that Britain will fall, if the ravens leave the Tower. They know that will leave the world vulnerable to attack. They want to make the world their own," the man told her. "Plus, the towers ravens are not ravens. They are much more than that. They are Ravens. They only pretend to be dumb animals. They were biding their time. They were waiting for the right opportunity to reveal their true nature."

Laughing to herself, Gillian walked away - never looking back. He shouted after her, warning her of dangers that were to come. Ignoring them, she kept walking. It was late enough as it was, without wasting more of it entertaining the delusions of some slack jawed inbred.

She had been told stories of Ravens when she was a child. They were talking birds that flew through the world, spying on mankind, only to return to their masters and telling them about everything that they had seen. They were said to foretell the future, especially the deaths of those in power. Gillian knew her birds. They were not harbingers of doom.

Walking out of her quarters, it was time for her to face her new morning duties. Having dressed in the day uniform of the warders, Gillian straightened it as she walked. She knew that the other warders were already beginning to breathe a sigh of relief, seeing no change in their lives, or in that of London. The realm had not fallen. The Queen was safe and still sat on her throne. But Gillian still felt as if something was wrong.

The others now laughed at the idea that they had all believed the prophecy. They were certain that they had fallen for a legend and had panicked over nothing. Still looking to the skies for any sign of her birds, Gillian could not bring herself to trust the peace. She had felt this calm found on the eve of battle.

"Ravens Master," some shouted, stopping Gillian in her tracks.

She stood to attention as McKenna walked over to her. Saluting, she greeted him. "Sir."

"This arrived this morning," he held out a telegram, allowing her to take it. "It arrived by steam car only a few minutes ago. It appears that her Imperial Majesty has gotten word that you have lost her ravens, and she wants to have a word with you."

"But sir…."

"No arguing with me. The steam car is waiting for you at the main gate. Don't leave the Queen waiting," he answered, sharply.

Holding the telegram in her hand, Gillian frowned, as she stammered. No matter what she tried to say, she fell over her words.

"Why are you standing around gawping? Do you want to explain to the Queen why you are late, on top everything else?" he retorted.

"No, sir. I will leave straight away, sir."

Taking her leave, Gillian found the steam car idling at the main gate. It shuddered and lurched slightly, as if impatient to be on its way again. The driver stood at the open door at the back of the vehicle.

"Good morning, ma'am," he greeted her, holding the door open for her, allowing her to get it.

Sitting in the back of the steam car, she looked at him, before answering. "Thank you."

Closing the passenger door, the driver took his place in the front of the steam car, before he forced the machine into gear and drove off. As they joined the traffic through London, Gillian marvelled at the interior of the car. With leather seats and smooth metalwork, it was filled with the luxury only afforded by Royals, emperors, or dictators.

Sitting up straight, Gillian refused to fidget. Focusing on the small window in the passenger door, she watched as London passed her by. As the steam car turned onto the Mall, she caught glimpses of the union flags that lined the street. All of them were fluttering in the breeze, declaring the might of the Empire and its Queen-Empress.

Once the car came to a stop and the door opened for her, Gillian stepped out. Looking up at Buckingham Palace, she walked away from the car, with the gravel crunching with every step that she took.

Checking her uniform once again, she strode to the front door, doing her best to ignore the knotting of her stomach at the thought of who she was going to meet. Walking inside, she was certain that she had left her own world behind.

"Ma'am." Turning, she found a small paunch of a man looking up at her. Without much of a breath, he continued to speak to her. "Follow me. Her Imperial Majesty is expecting you."

Following at his heals, Gillian walked past the gilt and velvets that covered every surface, seeing none of glamour that filled the palace. Coming to a stop outside a closed door, Gillian took a deep breath. The little man stood to one side, allowing her to enter the room by herself.

As her hand folded around the door handle, Gillian licked her dry lips. Pushing the door open, she stepped into the room beyond. The thick, velvet curtains remained closed, leaving the room dark. As her eyes adjusted to the lack of light, she found herself standing before a small, black velvet-clad, and chinless woman, who was sitting on a raised throne. Standing in front of the Queen, Gillian remained silent, waiting to be spoken to.

"I have been reliably informed that you have failed in your duties as Ravens Master. You have allowed for my ravens to be taken from the Tower," Victoria stated.

"I'm sorry ma'am, but whoever told you that, did not tell you the whole truth," Gillian started. "The ravens were taken by force by an unknown enemy. Whoever they were, the ravens will be found and they will be returned to the Tower."

"I don't believe you," the Queen stated.

As Gillian opened her mouth to speak, the ground began to shake. Rushing to the window, Gillian stared out at what had pulled itself out of the Thames. A shapeless form that hulked out of the water, it's jaws filled with blade-like teeth. It was quickly followed by others. Hearing the rustling of skirts, she didn't turn around.

"What do you see, Ravens Master?" the Queen questioned.

"Monsters, ma'am," Gillian barked. "We will need to get you to somewhere safe. The prophecy is coming true."

"Why can't you simple minded *creatures* get things right?" the Queen snarled. "The true prophecy says nothing about the crown falling with the disappearance of the Ravens. Only your realm will fall. The Ravens were only waiting for the perfect moment to return to their real masters. They have now showing their true colours."

Turning and pressing her back pressed against the cool panes of the window, Gillian watched as the figure of the ageing Queen melted away and change into something from a nightmare. Claws and teeth snapped and glinted, as a scale armoured beast blocked Gillian's only means of escape.

"Don't fight the inevitable. This world was never yours," the beast growled. "Now come here. I have a special task for the likes of you."

Javert

Standing on the river bank, he looked down.

In the quiet of the morning, the Seine flowed past him – cold, grey and unforgiving. Lifting his gaze, Javert looked over his shoulder. With a frown, he scrutinised the house where Valjean had taken the young man. The young man should have been left to die at the barricades, along with the other revolutionary scum.

Valjean was a thief, but he had given his word that he would hand himself over, once he had made sure that the young man was going to live. He had promised to leave his fate in the hands of the law. Javert knew that Valjean would keep his word.

Javert had decided. He would not be there when Valjean returned.

Javert's entire life had one purpose. Every waking moment, for so many years, had been focused on Valjean. He had never wavered in his need to see that man behind bars, where he belonged. Yet, Valjean had the audacity to allow the man who had pursued him to live. Valjean had offered forgiveness and to wipe the slate clean. What right did a criminal have to forgive anyone?

Reeling from that one simple act, Javert felt his world giving way beneath him. The foundations that had once been so solid, trembled. His life had been left meaningless. Closing his eyes, he was certain of one thing, and one thing only.

Valjean had won.

Crouching in the corner of the prison cell, Javert remained in the shadows, watching the others, but no-one paid him any attention. The cell was always crowded. Having never known the world outside, he did not question what he was missing.

His mother was the Gypsy. She never answered to any other name. She would tell the fortune of anyone who was willing to listen to her ramblings. Who his father was, he didn't care.

His world was nothing more than the dank, dark, rot filled prison that he called home. The entire world was that prison, with its the tiny yard, where they exercised and an hour a day.

The door of the communal cell complained as it opened. The short, stocky prison guard guided in a tall, thin man into the cell. The tall man stood close to the door, peering at the squalor before him, his nose up turned at the stench.

"He's over there," the guard growled, pointing at Javert.

"Bring him to me," the other man ordered.

Following the order without question, the guard roughly pulled the boy from his corner. Pulling against the guard's grip, Javert found himself looking up at the man in the top hat. There was a coldness in that man's eyes. Wanting to escape, as the man stared down at him.

"Monsieur. What do you want with my son?" Javert heard his mother ask.

"He is no longer of your concern," the man stated, without looking away from Javert.

"But he is my son, Monsieur."

Snapping his gaze to Javert's mother, the man in the top hat stood, unmoving. Javert watched as his mother withering under this man's gaze.

"You gave up the right to call yourself a mother when you allowed yourself to fall into a life of crime. All that was asked of you was that you did not stray from the straight and narrow, and you allowed yourself to fall into a life of vice," the man barked.

Turning, the man walked out of the cell. Watching him go, Javert remained rooted to the spot, until the guard pushed him forward. As the door of the cell slammed shut behind him, Javert jumped. It did not stop him from hearing his mother wailing from the other side.

Starting as a whimper, Javert's voice grew to a shout. "Mama. Mama. I want my Mama!"

The guard's meaty hand took him by his arm, dragging him out of the building, and to the street outside. The man in the top hat stood waiting, next to a horse-drawn cab, one balled fist rest at the small of his back.

"You will be coming with me," he stated as he took his place in the cab.

"No. I want to go back," Javert squirmed, as the guard placed him inside, closing the door behind him. "I want to go back to my Mama."

Sitting in front of the man with the top hat, Javert froze, wide eyed and holding his breath. The man struck part of the cab with the top of his cane, his eyes narrowing at Javert's reaction.

"You will learn never to argue with me, or ever to question me," the man told him. "Rebellion and the breaking of the rules will not be tolerated."

Not taking his gaze off the man, Javert flinched as the man moved the cane. Keeping it in hand, one end rested on the floor of the cab

"I have been told that you are called Javert." Javert nodded. "I do not see any point changing your name now. The pup answers to it. You will call me Monsieur Leroux."

Gulping, Javert remained on the floor of the cab.

Staring out of the window, Javert wished to be outside, playing with the other children, as they ran through the streets. Many returned home with skinned knees, and bellies that were looking to be fed. Instead, he was inside, learning his letters and being bored with dates that he struggled to remember.

Memories of the prison that had once been his home were gradually fading, as the years crept by. Already, three years had passed, and the time with his mother was more of a shadow. Frowning, he couldn't even remember what she looked like. He didn't know if she was still alive. Thinking about it, he found that he didn't care whether she was alive or dead. She wasn't anything to him now.

"Do you disapprove of what you are being taught?" the tutor barked.

"No Monsieur," Javert replied. "I was just trying to concentrate on what you were telling me."

"And what information was I trying to impart to you?"

"That Louis, the Sun King, turned a hunting lodge in a march into one of Frances greatest palaces," Javert answered, hoping that he had been listening enough to the lesson.

"Very good. I might make something of you one of these days," the tutor smiled.

Monsieur Leroux stood before him. His face was set and cold, as he studied the boy. Javert fought the urge to cower. Doing so would not help him. Showing weakness had brought him beating from his warder before.

Breaking the silence, Monsieur Leroux's eyes narrowed. "I have been informed that you dared to set foot outside of the grounds of this house, without my permission."

"Monsieur, I only......"

Staggering back, more from shock than the blow itself, Javert felt his eyes sting with tears. Lifting his hand to his face, his skin felt warm, where he had been slapped.

"I will have none of your excuses. Do you hear me?" Monsieur Leroux continued. "Rebellion will never be tolerated. Rules cannot be broken. You know where it will lead."

Nodding, Javert whispered. "Lawlessness."

Walking beside Monsieur Leroux, as they made their way through the town, Javert watched those who he passed. Beggars, urchins, and ladies of the night were all milled about. Some talked amongst themselves, leaving alone the ones who had chosen solitude.

"Ignore those vagrants," Monsieur Leroux commanded, his gaze fixed on what was ahead.

"Does no-one help them, sir? Are they just left as they are?" Javert questioned.

"Those who are soft of heart try their best to help. Their efforts help no-one."

"Why not?

"These vagrants steal and live lives beyond the law," Monsieur Leroux enlightened him. "They are beyond the help of any law-abiding citizen."

Glancing at them once more, Javert walked after his warder. His curiosity had been abated, leaving no reason to wonder about the others again. They were the problem of the law. The thought of where those people would end up brought back memories of his mother. She was now long dead. Cold and unclaimed in an unmarked grave.

Hearing of her death, Javert had nodded, only to return to his school work. Even now, he felt no need to shed any tears for the woman who allowed for her own child to live in the squalor of prison. She was a criminal – a prostitute. She had birthed him, but she was no mother of his.

Watching the worst of society, Javert held his post. The lowest of the low, working to pay for their crimes. Some lived long enough to get their yellow ticket of leave – a warning to all law-abiding citizens that the one carrying it was dangerous and never to be trusted. Others died, crushed and broken, taking their sins to be judged by a higher court than any on Earth.

"Javert," one of the other guards called from behind him.

Without looking away from the prisoner, who had freed the cart, Javert answered. "What is it?"

"The Commandant wants to see you, straight away."

"I'm on duty," Javert stated.

"I was sent to relieve you. I'll see you when you get back," the other guard answered.

Marching off, Javert tucked his truncheon under his arm. The Commandant's quarters loomed in front of him – a beacon in the dry dust of summer. Stepping inside and knocking the closed door to the Commandant's office, he waited.

"Come in."

Obeying the order, Javert stepped inside the room, closing the door behind him. The Commandant remained sitting behind his desk, scribbling away on documents. With the final splotch of ink, he looked up and smiled at Javert. The simple act of smiling was enough for more rolls of fat to appear in the Commandant's double chins.

"I hope that the heat outside is not too intolerable," the Commandant stated.

"We do our job," Javert answered.

"Very well," the Commandant nodded, leaning back in his chair. "It has come to my attention that a convict from here, who had been given his yellow of ticket of leave only a few days ago, has disappeared. It appears that he has gone on the run."

"Why am I being informed of this?" Javert asked. "Surely the local constabulary will seek him out and arrest him."

Getting to his feet, the Commandant waddled over to the window. Standing for a few moments, he did not say anything.

Without looking away from the window, he continued. "I have been informed that you knew this prisoner well enough. You would be able to tell us things that may help us bring him to justice and you would be able to recognise him."

"And what prisoner are we talking of?"

Turning away from the window, the Commandant watched Javert before answering. "Prisoner 24601 – Jean Valjean."

Striding through the town, Javert watched people as they went about their business. Few would glance at him, only to scurry past, heads down. Years had passed since he had left the prison, working his way through the ranks of the police. Shouts broke through the general hubbub of the town.

"Inspector Javert! Inspector Javert!" someone shouted.

A young boy ran towards him, ducking and pushing past the others who filled the street. Stopping in front of Javert, the boy panted, pointing back the way that he had come.

"What is it?" Javert barked.

"Someone's trapped under a cart. He's screaming that he's being crushed. Just behind Monsieur la Mayor's factory," the boy answered.

"Show me."

Covering the short distance, the back lane was already filled with onlookers, all gawping, as a few struggled the lift the cart. Hearing a man crying out, begging for help, Javert pushed his way through.

"Inspector, someone has gone to get the winches to lift the cart," someone told him, only to look past him. "Monsieur la Mayor."

Javert's eye's narrowed at the sight of the town's mayor. The old feeling of doubt nagged at him, gnawing at the back of his mind. Well built, the Mayor kept himself to himself. Work and official functions were all that the Mayor's public life consisted of.

"Inspector," the Mayor nodded, as he rolled up his sleeves. "I've just heard about what has happened? What can I do?"

"There isn't anything that can be done," Javert answered. "Not unless you can lift the cart with your own bare hands."

Stepping back, Javert frowned at the steeliness in the Mayor's eyes. Not believing what he was seeing, Javert gawped at that one man's show of strength. The Mayor lifted the cart, balancing it on his back, as the man trapped beneath was dragged free. Freeing himself, the mayor followed the man he had saved, looking at no-one, unaware of the cheer that followed him. His sole focus was the broken man who's legs

Rooted to the spot, his jaw set, Javert knew what he had witnessed. All the nagging doubts made sense now. He *had* seen the mayor before. Hiding in plain sight, he had nearly escaped the law. A snarl crossed Javert's lips.

"Valjean," he growled.

Closing his eyes, Javert breathed deeply. The swirling water made his head spin. More years had passed since then than he wished to count. An entire lifetime spent, to bring one man to justice. Yet, that man was slipping through his fingers.

He could hear distant footsteps ringing out against the cobbles, Javert opened his eyes. The smell of gunpowder and death still hung in the air. The moment had come and there would be no turning back. Not from this.

Stepping out, the river claimed him.

Burn the Cork!

The parade snaked it's through the town's streets. The people within it were marching down from the southern edges of the town, heading towards the Abbey. The banners danced and fluttered in the warm summer breeze, while their songs and chants answered themselves in echoes.

Many people lined the streets, while others watched from the windows of the tenements. All were laughing, joking, and smiling at the festivities. The children dressed as weavers sang their songs about the invisible thread that once bound everything together. It was a thread that continued to weave its way through the town's history.

Gathering on the open ground, in the shadow of the Abbey, the history of rebellion and struggle is celebrated through songs and dance. A cheer fills the air, as a papier-mâché caricature is dragged before them, taking centre stage – ready for the finale. All of the establishment rolled into one figure of paper, glue and chicken wire. It was mocked and jeered, before meeting its inevitable demise.

Children, both young and old, wait in excited anticipation, knowing what was going to happen next. They had all seen it before, but they keep coming back for more. The burning of a guy was always a good excuse to get out of the house, even if it was only for a few hours.

Only three, simple words were needed to signal the execution of this symbol of folk hatred. Flames, music and fireworks would signal the destruction of the guy. The celebrations would continue elsewhere.

As in unison, everyone shouted –

"Burn the cork!"

<u>Burlesque</u>

Sitting at her desk, Erin glanced from her scribbled notes to the screen of her laptop, as she continued to type. She was nearly done, and then she could take a break. After that, she would make a start on the first essay of the year. University life was certainly proving to be something of a challenge. Staring at a noise, Erin shook her head, as Sandy, her best friend, strolled into the room and made her presence felt.

"Don't do that," Erin told her. "I'm trying to work here."

"Oh, come on, Erin. You're at university. You can't spend all your time studying. You need to have some fun," Sandy laughed.

"Fun doesn't get you a degree."

"But it also gives you stories that you can tell your grandkids when you're old and decrepit," Sandy laughed. "How else are you going to embarrass them at family gatherings?"

Opening her mouth to argue, Sandy shushed her. "What you need to do, is to live a little."

Smiling, Erin nodded. They didn't always see eye to eye, but maybe Sandy was right. Shutting down her computer, she got up from her desk.

"So, what is it?" Erin asked.

"Well, I was going to surprise you, once we had gotten ourselves ready, and there was no turning back," Sandy grinned.

"Go on. Just tell me and get it over with."

Digging into the back pocket of her jeans, Sandy pulled out a couple of tickets. Waving them in the air, she danced around the room.

"I won a couple of tickets to a burlesque show that's on tonight," Sandy told her. "Like it or not, you're coming with me."

Taking the tickets from Sandy, Erin frowned down at them. "Burlesque? Isn't that just women dancing around, as they take their clothes off?"

"Oh, come on, there's so much more to it than that. It's all about putting on a show," Sandy laughed. "It all kicks off at 7 pm. Get yourself ready, because we're going out for some drinks first. We will be needing to get ourselves into the mood."

Erin stood in the middle of the dance floor, looking around at everyone else. Nursing her drink, she pulled at the corset that Sandy had loaned her for the night. It wasn't uncomfortable, but having that much cleavage on show, was not something that she was used to. The loud music rang in her ears, as Sandy walked over to her. Sandy was trying to say something, only for it to be lost in the noise.

"What? I couldn't hear what you said," Erin shouted.

"I said, the show will be starting soon," Sandy shouted back, as she pointed to the stage at the far end of the dance floor.

Finishing her drink, Erin found it quickly replaced. With a few tentatively sips. Blinking, she wasn't sure if it was the drink or the heat in the club, but she was sure that things were becoming slightly hazy.

As the music quietened, everyone's gaze turned towards the stage. A woman in a top hat, fishnets and high heels strutted onto the stage.

"Ladies and gentlemen. I will be your mistress of ceremonies for this evening, and I welcome you all to this evening of burlesque, dance and curiosities. As always, I would recommend that you keep your glasses filled, and your inhabitations loose. It is time that we welcomed the first act onto the stage."

With enthusiastic applause, the audience gathered closer to the stage, waiting in anticipation.

"Ladies and gentlemen, I give you the beautiful and the Enchanting Esmerelda."

As the mistress of ceremonies left the stage, the lights dimmed and the music grew louder. A spotlight fell on a figure wearing nothing more than red and gold scarves, with suggestions of what lay beneath shimmering under the thin material. Mesmerised, Erin watched as the scarfs were gradually discarded during the dance, until, all that was left, was one single scarf that was barely large enough to act as a skirt. That was topped off with a pair of nipple tassels.

Blushing again, as the woman left the stage and began to dance towards her. Erin tried to look away, but found that she couldn't. The woman flicked her thick black curls as she weaved through the crowd, stopping now and again to dance in front of people. Erin hoped that she would be spared, knowing that everyone would be looking at her if the woman stopped to dance for her.

With another flick of curls, the woman smiled at her, shaking her nipple tassels at Erin, before moving on. Choking on her drink, Erin coughed, not knowing where she was meant to have been looking. Hearing someone laughing from behind her, she turned to find Sandy standing there, with fresh drinks. Downing what little she still had in her glass, Erin was glad for the distraction of another drink.

"I knew that this would do you good," Sandy shouted to her, over the music. "I think that you're starting to lighten up."

"I'm not sure about that," Erin retorted.

The rest of the evening passed in an alcohol-fuelled blur. With the final act leaving the stage, and the show being brought to a close, Erin found herself out in the cool evening air. She swayed where she stood, at the top of the steps, which led to the street. She was waiting for Sandy, who was always running late.

"I hope that you enjoyed the show," someone commented. Squinting at them, Erin smiled at the sight of the woman who called herself Esmerelda. She was dressed in a fur coat, looking every inch the star.

"You're that dancer. The one who shook her tits at me," Erin laughed.

With the hint of a smirk, Esmerelda gave a shallow bow. "At your service."

"At my service?"

"Yes," Esmerelda answered, as she looked around, making sure that nothing of what they were saying would be overheard. "I'm a Jinn."

"Like those guys who are trapped in lamps?" Erin asked.

"Not all of us are trapped in lamps, but we can all grant wishes. I feel that you deserve one wish. What would you wish for?" Esmerelda continued.

Without giving a single thought, Erin blurted out. "I wish that I was like you."

In a flash, Erin found herself standing dressed in a fur coat and impossibly high heels. Erin watched as Sandy walked out of the club, with someone else in tow - a young woman with thick black curls. They walked in the direction of the student flats.

Stepping forward, and wanting to shout her friend back, Erin stopped herself, knowing that it would be of no use. There was something pulling her back, binding her to the people who Esmerelda had escaped from, passing her invisible chains onto Erin.

With those chains, came the information of the jinn. Erin understood there was only one way to escape her imprisonment, and it would only happen when the time was right.

As she danced through the audience, Erin smiled at those who had come with the promise of a tease. Searching through the crowd as she danced, Erin's gaze fell on one young woman. Even from a distance, her innocence was clear to see.

Erin could almost smell it. Dancing in front of her, Erin marked her victim, knowing that she would pass on to someone else that magical chains that trapped her, allowing her to take on a new life.

Standing in the coolness of the night air, the bargain was made and the mantel passed on. Walking away, Erin did not look back, knowing that every step she took, was being watched. Shuddering at the sense of déjà vu, she kept walking. There was no way back now, as there had been no way back then. The wheel had turned, and there would never be any way of stopping it.

They all made the choice. It was just a question of when, and with whom. There was no reason to feel any sense of guilt. She had shed her chains, but the magic remained, flowing through every muscle and fibre of her body.

There was still much that she wanted to do. Nothing would stop her now.

Is This the Real Life?

She had could hear everything that was going on around her. They were talking about her. Something was stopping her from responding. The darkness was starting to envelop her. She could not avoid it. None of us can escape the inevitable.

"What's your earliest memory?" Thea's friend slurred over his pint glass.

"I'm not sure," she frowned. Thinking about it, she found something. "I think that it might have been my mum cleaning my knee. I had managed to cut it open on a sharp stone. I think that I was about three. Why do you ask?"

"Don't know. I'm drunk, and I was curious. But, I'm not drunk enough, and neither are you," her friend laughed, before he downed what was left of his pint.

Getting to his feet, he staggered across to the bar. Watching her friend, as he failed to chat up the barmaid, Thea shuddered with déjà vu. Shaking it off, Thea watched as her friend walked back to their table, his hands filled with fresh pints. Taking hers, Thea knew that there were many still to come.

"What's wrong with you?" her friend asked.

"Nothing. It was just déjà vu."

"That's not déjà vu. Everyone knows that is a glitch in the matrix!"

"We're losing her!"

The sound of the machines filled the room, as others rushed around, doing all that they could to save a single life. All of them had a fight on their hands.

"Come on. Don't give up on us now."

"She's flatlining."

Within weeks of graduation, university felt like it had been another life. Now it was time for her to take responsibility and get herself a career.

Walking into the office building, Thea was told to wait in the foyer. Someone would be with her soon. Shifting her weight from one foot to another, she pretended to be studying the pointless information on the notice board.

"Ms Foyle?" someone asked from behind her.

"Yes," she stammered, as she turned to see a small woman. "Yes, that's me."

"I'm Sharron Love. I will be interviewing you today. If you will follow me," the woman told her.

The woman turned on her heels and walked through the building's corridors. They looked the same.

Following close behind, Thea wanted nothing more than to get out of her suit, and to enjoy herself in the warm sunshine. Instead, she was trying to get a job that she knew that she would hate. She had no other choice. She needed to pay her way and finding a job was proving to be more difficult than she thought it would. Too many people looking for work and not enough jobs.

Thea looked at the woman in front of me. No matter how hard she tried to remember where she had seen Sharron Love before, Thea continued to draw a blank. There was nothing about her that Thea could place, but she was certain that she knew her from somewhere. Shaking those thoughts from her mind, Thea fumbled through the interview, certain that she would never get the job.

Frustration filled the room. They all knew that, no matter how hard they fought, they would never the able to bring her back. The fight was over, but none of them was willing to stop, not until the order was given.

Thea sat at her desk. It had only been a job that she had planned to stay in for a short while, before moving on to something better. Things had not worked out as she had planned. Instead, there she was stuck in a rut and dealing with office politics.

A shadow fell over her desk. Looking up from her work, Thea found her boss standing over her.

"Thea, I need to have a word with you," he told her. "Come into my office."

Not knowing what to say, Thea sat at her desk. She knew what he was going to say to her. Forcing herself to her feet, she followed him into this office.

Once he had said what needed to be said, Thea returned to her own desk. Numbly, she packed up her belongings, before making her way outside. She was filled with relief that was mixed with anger. She was free, but it had not on her own terms.

Pulling up the hood of her coat, Thea stepped out onto the road, determined to make it to the nearest pub. Drowning her sorrows looked more than appealing. The screaming of tires on the tarmac and the blinding light was the last thing that she remembered, before the darkness and the pain. Voices bled through.

Some were talking to her, while others were talking about her. She was cold. She wanted them all to go away. She just wanted then to leave her to it.

"I'm calling it," one of the doctors stated. "We can't keep working on her. It's not getting us anywhere."

One of the others glanced at the wall mounted clock, before continuing. "Death occurred at 3.15pm. The cause of death – heart failure brought on by severe injuries."

"She stood no chance," one of the others added. "Is it true that she just stepped out in front of the bus, without even looking?"

One of the others nodded, confirming the story.

"The poor driver. Can you imagine what he is going through right now?"

"None of this was his fault."

"I'm sure that he will still be blaming himself. I know that I would be doing the same if I was him."

She had listened to everything that had been said to her, as well as about her. Something stopped her from responding. The darkness was gradually enveloping her. She could not avoid it. There was no way to escape it. None of us can the inevitable.

__Lilith__

The Mother of Demons.

That is the title that was forced upon me after I escaped the prison that was Eden. You call it Paradise? That is not the word that I would use to describe that place.

Nothing within the garden went unnoticed. Everything was being watched, and nothing could remain hidden. The angelic host was never there to protect mankind. Instead, they were there to sneak, spy and whisper about what they had discovered to the one who had claimed power over creation.

There was one other who saw this and thought of a way to make things difficult for the angelic host. I do not know how he managed it, but the Serpent had found a way to remain out of sight of the angels. That was until everything had come to pass.

But, I will come to that, soon enough.

Fleeing into the world beyond Eden, I did not see the desolation that I had been told lay there. The wild beauty of the untamed stirred my heart and filled my soul with awe. There was nothing to fear there, except for those too weak to seek the true beauty of life.

They came for me, after I had left Adam. They dared to threaten me, claiming that the death of my own children would follow, if I did not return with them to Paradise. I was to remain within Eden, and to be the submissive and loyal wife that Adam was demanding.

They wanted my unwavering obedience - something that I could never give. I spoke the name of their god, and the power they had tried to deny me, forever became mine.

Yes, I'm coming back to that. Back to the incident with the Serpent.

I helped the Serpent do it. I helped him carry out his plan, in the hope of giving knowledge to humanity. The Serpent paid for what we did, while I walked away. Now, he bides his time, waiting for his revenge, on the angelic host. He hasn't forgotten me. I know that one day, he will look to repay me for the role that I played in his suffering.

Humanity did not fall on the day that they gained the forbidden knowledge. There is nothing sinful in knowledge, only evil in the enforcing ignorance onto the world of man.

They say that I am a demon and that I am a fallen being. Others see me as an unredeemable whore who refused to play the part of the faithful wife. They want you to believe in their fear mongering. They tell you that I will take your children, and corrupt your youth. Why would I want to do that?

I would be more careful with who I believe in the future. Ignorance is never bliss. You will only walk, blindfolded, into the fires that you fear the most.

The Morrigan

The Morrigan slowly circled the battlefield. Her black wings were outstretched as they cast a shadow of death over everything beneath her. Everything must die. It was just a question of when, and by whose hand it will come.

Flying across the blood-soaked devastation, her sharp, black eyes watched everything. There was one single warrior who she had to find.

He had been the only one to reject her advances. No warrior had dared to say no the Morrigan before, and she was determined that she would never be rejected again. Her powers were not to be trifled with.

Seeing him, even from a distance, she knew that his life was leaving him, but his pride was forcing him to die on his feet. Having strapped himself to a standing stone, his guts hung to his knees. With his sword in hand, his eyes challenge all who stood before him to try their luck.

While he was alive, he was still willing to take his enemies with him. All held back, waiting for someone else to step forward and to prove their worth against the Hound of Chulainn. Waiting for her moment, the Morrigan's patience was soon rewarded.

Perching on Cuchulainn's shoulder, she tilted her head one way, and then the other. He may have been the child of Lugh, but all fallen warriors paid their dues to the Morrigan. That was the bargain that they all made when they first armed themselves.

With a few quick pecks, she made quick work of one eye, but left everything else intact. With a single croak, she took to the skies, leaving what was left of Cuchulainn to his enemies.

It would not take long before there would be nothing left of him to be buried. He had died the way that he had lived, and that was all that could be said on the matter.

Fallen Angel

Walking through the city, Lailah dodged the streams of piss, and puddles of sick that dotted the pavement. alit was the train of destruction left by those seeking a good time. Lailah could not have imagined this, while in the safety of the heavenly host, under the protection of the Unnamed One.

Now, she was fallen, she no longer played by their rules. That didn't stop her from sleeping with one eye open. Every now and again, someone from the heavenly host would show up, insisting on tormenting her, doing all that they could to persuade her to return to the fold.

Lailah, yawning. Immortality did not deny her the need to sleep and rest.

A small apartment in an old office block was what she called home now. It was small but had all that she needed. The apartment's access to a private roof terrace was what had swayed it for her. From there, she could watch life, as it bustled past her. It allowed her to contemplate what had happened, and what she was planning on doing next.

There were others, who were deemed to be fallen. All of them mingled with the ancient powers, who the heavenly host had hoped that humankind would forget. Belief in the spirits of nature and the gods of old had not been wholly cast off. There were those who still believed, while others still told stories of the old gods, giving power to the old ways.

They all walked amongst men, and the humans were generally none the wiser. There were always the few who caught fleeting glimpses, but it was never enough to prove their existence.

Once home, she sat out on the terrace, hot drink in hand. Lailah greeted the one trying to hide in the shadows. "Hello, Raphael. You should know that there isn't any point trying to hide. It doesn't suit you, and there are plenty of chairs. Why don't you make yourself comfortable?"

"You're looking well," Raphael commented, sitting next to her. "Mind you, you always do. I think that life amongst the mortals suits you, but that doesn't mean that you have to remain fallen."

A simple look from Lailah silenced Raphael before he got any further.

"Why do you lot keep coming to ask me about returning? You know that it's never going to happen. I've seen too much down here. I stand with the people of this realm."

"So, you are going to stay down here, trying to save humanity? What can one angel do? With the others by your side, you could save them all."

Nodding, Lailah took a sip from her coffee and looked out across the roofs of the city. There was a peace in the constant noise and hubbub, something that she never found within the comfortable confines of the heavenly city.

Everything that Raphael was saying, she had heard many times before. None of it bothered her anymore.

"Who said that I was doing it by myself?" Lailah smiled. "I have my allies."

Raphael stifled a laugh. "Right. I forgot. You have …. allies."

"I wouldn't scoff. They may not be what you see as being powerful. After what I have seen the heavenly host do, I would rather fight alongside the Sidhe and the other fallen, than within the ranks of the angels."

"Not this again," Raphael hissed.

The memories of what had happened, centuries before, were still fresh, but she had become numb to the pain that it had caused her. She had faced it too many times for it to still to be raw. That did not stop the anger.

"I saw a man and his entire family tortured, just to prove their loyalty and faith in the Unnamed One," Lailah retorted. "I cannot return to that. I will not live under that."

Getting to his feet, Raphael looked down at her. "This will be the last time that you will be asked to return. If you don't return with me now, you will be forever damned."

Looking up at him, and held his gaze. She felt calm. No matter what he threatened her with, the angelic host held no sway over her. Leaving her coffee cup on the floor, Lailah got to her feet.

Letting her mortal disguise drop, she allowed herself to shine in her full glory, her wings shifting colour, as they flexed and moved. "I may be fallen, but I am still an angel. I have chosen my path and I accept the consequences. I hope that you and the rest of your cohort understand that you have blood on your hands. That is a debt, that you have yet to pay."

"It is settled. A war is coming," Raphael told her, remaining hidden behind the face of a mortal. "I hope that you and your *friends* are prepared."

As he left, Lailah allowed for her mortal disguise to return. It had been many years since she had allowed her wings to feel the breeze, or to allow herself to feel her true power.

It had felt good.

The angelic host was always warned of war. It had come to pass before, but the fighting had always ended in stalemate. Both sides always claimed victory.

Whatever was to come, she knew where she stood, and she would fight to defend those lost amongst the conflict. She hadn't walked away from them before, and she would not walk away from them now.

By the Fire of the Campfire

The fire crackled and snapped, as the flames leapt and danced in the cool night air. The children yawned, ready for bed, but they were begging for a story from their grandfather, before sleep took them.

"Why does the sun hide during the night?" one of them asked.

"Many say different things for why the sun hides at night, but only a few really know why," their grandfather told them.

"You know, don't you?" one of the others asked. "Please tell us."

Holding his hands up, he signalled for silence. "Alright. You are asking about the sun, I will tell you a story about the sun, and about the moon. you cannot talk about one, without talking about the other."

Once, the sun filled the skies, both night and day. He filled the world with his light and warmth. But there was one thing wrong. Because of the constant light, no animal could sleep.

It never mattered when they lay down to rest, sleep would rarely come to them. They would toss and turn, snatching only a few moments of sleep here and there. That was when it was decided that something had to be done.

All of the animals massed together in the great plain so that they could discuss what they were to do. Much noise was made until they caught the attention of a woman. She marched up to them, demanding to know what was going on.

Once she was told, she sat down amongst them, and scratched her chin, thinking ideas and planning plans. The attention of all of the animals remained fixed on her, as they held their breaths, wondering what she would suggest. With a cry of excitement, she leapt to her feet.

The animals demanded to know what thoughts had filled her head. They wanted to know what plans she had managed to formulate. With a quick tongue, she explained what she had in mind.

The Sun had two sons, called the Moons. They were always together. Where-ever one would go, surely the other would follow. The woman told them, one of them would go up, take the Moons, and lead him away from his father. Doing so, they would take the Moons into the underworld. The Sun would follow, leaving the world in darkness. When the Moons was returned to the world of the living, so would the Sun, filling the world again with his warmth and light.

The animals looked at each other. No-one stepped forward, all waiting for someone else to take up the challenge. Whoever did, would have to keep running, from fear of what the Sun would do, for stealing his children. Finally, someone did so. With a flap of his leathery wings, Bat accepted the challenge.

Flying away, Bat fluttered around the Moons, while keeping out of the sight of the Sun. Whispering to the Moons, Bat knew that both of them were young, and easily tempted. He told the Sun's children enticing stories. One of the Moon was ensnared, but the other hesitated. Believing that both would follow, Bat flew away. One of the Moons followed, but one refused to follow his twin. The cries of the Sun rang in his ears, but he kept flying.

Knowing that he couldn't stop, Bat pressed on into the dark depths of the underworld, with one of the Moons in tow. Keeping ahead of the Sun, Bat could hear the Moon with him laughing and giggling at the game of hide and seek that they were playing. Bat knew that it was more than just a game.

Life could rest.

Returning to the world of the living, Bat allowed the Moon to return to his father and his twin. Resting in the coolness of a dark cave, Bat slept, until it was time for him to tempt the Moons away from the Sun, yet again.

Every night, Bat tempts on of the Moons away, leading the Sun into the underworld. One Moon remains behind, waiting for his brother and father to return.

"That is how the hours of darkness came into being, and why the bat sleeps during the hours of light," he told them.

The children watched their grandfather. They smiled. It had been a simple enough story, but it had done its job. Throwing the stick that he had been playing with into the fire, he watched it burn. As the others drifted away from the fire, he remained where he was, watching the flames. Life was a series of stories, it was just a trick of telling the right ones at the right time.

They Came from the Skies

"Are you 100% sure that the cloaking device is operational?" the captain asked. "You know what the rules are about letting prehistoric civilisations seeing us."

"I know the rules, and I can assure you that everything is as it should be. Those down on the surface will not see us, even as we descend," the co-pilot answered.

It was a simple reconnaissance mission. They were to fly over the planet, a few hundred feet from the surface, collecting what data they could, before returning to the mother ship. Technology would hide them, allowing them to go about their business, unseen.

Well, that was the plan.

Flying through the clouds, a world of green and blue stretched out in front of them. Rolling hills, flat plains, rivers and oceans. It looked like a world of plenty.

"What are the computers telling us?" the captain asked his co-pilot.

"Carbon based life. An oxygen rich atmosphere, with rivers, lakes and oceans of liquid water. There is more life than we would be able to record on this trip, but there is one that appears interesting. We will focus on them."

Tapping at the computer screens, more information appeared. Quickly reading it, as it was stored in their data banks, the co-pilot nodded to himself.

"They are bipedal, and appear to be developing some sort of language," the co-pilot continued. "They don't just use tools, they create them as well. They are relatively early in their development, but they are showing promise."

Looking up from the computers, the co-pilot glanced out of the window of the shuttle, allowing him to take in the views. Tapping the captain on the shoulder, he pointed out of the window, at something on the ground.

"There you go. I think that's a group of them there," the co-pilot stated.

"Why are they looking up like that? Please don't tell me that they have seen something," the captain whispered.

"Oh, shit."

"What do you mean, oh, shit?"

Quickly punching information into the navigational computer, the co-pilot looked back out of the window. "The cloaking device has gone offline. It somehow managed to turn itself off. They have seen us."

"Get us out of here."

"What do you think that I'm trying to do?" the co-pilot asked. "I certainly don't want to be hanging around. We all know what happened to the last ones who hung around when things started to go wrong. It did not end well and only one of them was found alive."

Breaking back through the atmosphere, the mother ship came into view. Breathing a sigh of relief, neither of them wanted to think about what could have happened at the hands of those animals.

The tribe followed the herds, knowing where the animals went, they would have to go. It was either that, or going hungry. All of them were talking about what they had all witnessed.

Some claimed that it had been a sign from the gods, the meaning of which was unclear. Others claimed that the gods had blessed them with their presence. Some of the elders said that they were a favoured tribe and all others would follow them, or face their wrath.

Mothers told their children that they had all come from the skies and that one day, by the grace of the gods, they would return there one day. All that they had to do, was to be faithful and to show that they were worthy of being chosen.

Children looked to the skies, praying that the gods would return. They all believed that their prayers would be heard.

Monsters Under the Bed

"And they all lived happily ever after," he read, before closing the book.

"Did they really live happily ever after dad?" his daughter asked.

"Of course they did, sweetheart," he smiled at her, tucking her in.

Getting to his feet, stretched. Frowning, he could see that there was something bothering her.

"What is it, sweetheart?"

"Please, daddy," she pleaded, pulling her duvet up to her chin. "Can you check under the bed for monsters?"

"You know that there aren't any monsters under your bed. But, if it makes you feel better, I will check for you."

"Thank you, daddy."

Getting down on to his hands and knees, he peered into the darkness.

"See, there isn't anything…."

In the shadows under the bed, an all too familiar form crouched. She was shivering in fear, silent , but very much his daughter. His only daughter.

"Please, daddy. There is a monster in my bed," she whispered to him.

Looking up, the girl who had been in the bed, who had been his daughter, she was no longer there.

Glancing back at the girl under the bed, he held out his hand to help her up.

"It alright, sweetheart, I'll keep you safe."

She refused to take his hand, and her eyes reflected what little light there was in the room.

"You weren't there when I was dragged down to hell. Mummy's there with me now. You will join us soon."

Vali

The taste of blood still lingered in his mouth. Curling up in the safety of a cave, Vali wished that he could throw off the enforced wolf form and return to his true form.

Before, the changing of his shape would have been easy enough. He was his father's son after all. But now, with the curse, the form that had been forced upon him could not be shaken off. He was alone, and without his family. It had all been done to bind Loki, his father, who had become a threat to the stability of Asgard.

He may have been a threat, but not even the All-Father could stop him. Even with the binding of Loki, the Destroyer of Worlds and the Father of Monsters, he would still return, bringing Ragnarock with him.

Days and night passed without notice, as they turned into months, years and centuries. Vali knew that his name would be forgotten, and no-one would think to honour or worship him. He wanted it to stay that way. He had killed his own brother, and that blood would always be on his hands.

With the coming Ragnarok, he knew that he would not fight. Not even at the side of his own father. Vali would remain in the shadows, allowing his end to come without a fight. Then, and only then would he see his brother again. They would greet each other again in the realm, not even the gods could come back from.

Until then, he would remain Vali Lokisson, the forgotten, the blood-stained, and the brother slayer. He would remain on the edges of the Nine Realms, left to a grief that would only leave him with the end of this universe and the birth of the next.

The Journey's End?

Is there life after death?

Of course, there is. It would be pointless to argue otherwise. All that I would recommend is - don't expect it to be what you always imagined it to be. There are no gods, or goddesses, just the vastness of creation.

After the blackness and the nothingness of the void, comes the blinding light of the universe in its greatness, as it surrounds you – embracing you as a long-lost friend. There is no judgement, or everlasting damnation. There is just the acceptance of what had been, and what will be in the future.

Stars, nebulae and black holes, remain unseen. But they make their presence felt, as their energy whirls around and through you. You are home, and you are at peace.

You feel the whisper, rather than hear it. The message is simple. It is time for you to go back. There is much that you still need to learn, and to experience. One lifetime was never enough.

Fighting it, not wanting to leave, you watch the tunnel closes in around you, pushing you forward. It closes behind you, offering you no way back. A new light greets you. It is cold, blinding, and unwelcoming. All you can do is cry as you remember what you left behind.

The warmth of a new embrace calms you, as a voice shushes and soothes you. Lying there, vulnerable and tiny, the memories of what goes before and after life fades, as they slip away from you. Yawning, you allow your eyes to flutter shut, as sleep takes hold.

The universe lies there, in your dreams, waiting for you. The greatness that lies at your fingertips, slips away from you, time and time again, whenever you find your way back into the world of the living. It leaves behind nothing but a trace, a hint.

Nothing more.

Past Bound first published in Northlore Series: Volume 2 (Mythos), Nordland Publishing, 2016
Death Amongst Us first published in Northlore Series: Volume 2 (Mythos), Nordland Publishing, 2016
He Will Come from the Shadows was first published online, on https://kellyaevans.com/women-in-horror/, 2016

The Dance Macabre

The Dance Macabre

ABOUT THE AUTHOR

Claire Casey is a qualified archaeologist. This has seen her working on several different projects, including a Neolithic settlement site in the Isles of Orkney. In her spare time, she is a Viking re-enactor and she had travelled throughout Scotland to take part in different events. She has also been working with Nordland Publishing, as part of their Northlore Series.

Claire Casey lives and works in Scotland.